CONJURE

PRAISE FOR MARK WEST

"His crisp, economic style reels you straight in, and the horror hits you hard and quickly and refuses to lay off." — *Award-winning author and scriptwriter, Paul Finch*

Conjure: "A powerful and convincing piece of horror fiction" — *Gary McMahon, author of The Concrete Grove trilogy*

Conjure: "A strangely British tale, something that may have been produced in the seventies by Hammer or part of Tales of the Unexpected but very much updated with modern quotas of brutality and gore." — *Colin Leslie, The Black Abyss*

Conjure: "... is a great story with well-developed characters, and a great sense of place." — *Xomba*

The Mill: "...amongst the very best in the ghost story tradition." — *This is Horror*

In the Rain with the Dead: "...will grab you from page one and keep you in its clutches until the very last page! Mark West does what he does best — he scares the living daylights out of his readers!" — *author T. M. Gray*

In the Rain with the Dead: "You hear people say that they were '*sitting on the edge of their seats*'... That describes what it's like reading this book." — *Future Fire*

Strange Tales: "The bottom line is that if the stories in this collection do not scare you, they will disturb you. And if they do not disturb you, they will make you want to vomit." — *Rambles*

CONJURE

MARK WEST

First published by Rainfall Books 2009
Revised edition published 2013 by Greyhart Press
All Rights Reserved

ISBN: 978-1-909636-05-7

Also available in eBook editions

Greyhart Press

www.greyhartpress.com

In memory of my sister Tracy, who always believed (1971 - 2003)

Thanks to:
Mum & Dad; Sarah, Chris, Lucy & Milly; Nick Duncan and Pauline
Weston; Sue Moorcroft; T.M. Gray; John B Ford and Steve Lines (for
taking a chance on this in the first place); The Terror Scribes and the
FantasyCon bunch; Gary McMahon for the cover quote and the support;
and my pre-readers (Sarah, Nick, Terri, Laura "Flo" Brooks, David Roberts,
Mike & Melanie Pateman and Darren Franz).

Of course, as always, many thanks must go to Alison, who helped me
through this with love, kindness and laughter and Matthew, my Dude, who
always makes my day brighter.

CHAPTER 1

BETH HAMMOND PUSHED OPEN the door of Branigan House and stepped into the stale heat of Kingsway. It was early September, but the sun was warm and glared off the windows across the street, facts that had been masked to her all day by blinds and air-conditioning.

It was a quarter past five and she'd had a boring day training the temp to cover reception at Ann Lesley Training ("Good morning, Ann Lesley Training, how may I help you?" got monotonous when you said it all day and listening to someone else say it, as you mouthed the words, was painful). She couldn't wait to get home, because that meant packing and the holiday.

She and Rob couldn't afford to go away this year, so this break was much needed – though Rob had wanted to go somewhere hot. As far as Beth was concerned, so long as she escaped London and its awful contained heat and the debris of their lives at the moment, it didn't matter where they went.

Pete, one of the building's security guards, came across the street towards her, carrying a McDonald's bag and drinks tray. "See you tomorrow, love."

"You won't," Beth said and held the door open for him, "I'm off to Heyton."

Pete smiled, nodding his head. "That's a nice place, we went there every summer when the kids were small."

"I like it too."

"You take good care of yourself, you hear?"

"I will," she said and let the door swing shut. Standing with her back to the building, she rubbed her forehead and looked up and down Kingsway. Around her, people were making their way home, locked in their own thoughts and worries, their faces impenetrable masks, not wanting their fellow commuters to know who they were and what made them tick.

She knew how they felt; she looked like an office drone herself – her suit, her satchel with her lunchbox, paperback and copy of the *Express*, her handbag slung across her shoulder, her chestnut hair clean and pulled up. She looked all brisk and business-like, but it wasn't really her, just what everybody else would see. The ALT uniform was a knee-length navy blue skirt, a crisp white blouse (that was never white by the time she got home, or crisp in this heat), a poorly cut navy blue jacket, with the tiny ALT logo over her left breast, black shoes and no tights.

This was the Beth Hammond who turned up for work every morning at nine and spent her lunch break (thirty minutes and not a moment more) in the canteen on the fifth floor and was usually out of the building at about five-ish.

The real Beth Hammond didn't enjoy this life, but was resigned to the fact that it was just something else to make this a year to forget. It had started badly and didn't seem to be improving as the months moved forward, ageing and crinkling on the grand calendar of life.

Being a receptionist wasn't part of any life plan she'd made for herself but it paid the bills, most of them anyway. She'd wanted to get back into payroll, but the agency had placed her here and she enjoyed it at the beginning and stayed put. Things were going well, life was good with Rob, life was good in general and then, at the turn of the year, it had all started to crumble.

Just after Christmas, the company that Rob worked for – a decent job, a lot more money than he should have been paid according to a salary survey he'd read in *FHM*, nice offices – had downsized and their IT department was the first casualty. He'd temped for a while, managing to get himself so stressed that Beth was sure he was on the verge of a nervous breakdown – and how fun those few months had been – until he found a permanent job in the IT department of a travel agent's, troubleshooting files of people who could afford to buy timeshare in exotic locations.

Then, worst of all, was the news she'd heard a fortnight past Wednesday. Her mum had rung at work – which was unusual in itself and she knew that it'd be bad news – to say that Kathy, her cousin, had died in France. Beth had been close to Kathy when they were growing up and her disbelief about the whole situation meant that neither Hammond woman could make much sense of the other. The bulk of the news came out in another phone call, later in the evening, as Beth sat watching some crap on TV that only grabbed her attention through its whip crack editing and primary colour scheme.

Kathy seemed to have it all. She'd gone to university and breezed the four years, moved to Paris with an excellent job and found a handsome French husband. She and Beth kept in touch, often through email and whilst Kathy had seemed down recently, nothing was said outright, by either Beth or her, but it was there if you read between the lines. Maybe something should have been said, those few extra moments being enough to sort things out for Kathy, rather than having her feel there was no alternative but to take her own life.

The news had shaken Beth badly – she couldn't imagine how Kathy must have felt for suicide to be an option. What had gone so wrong for her, when she seemed to have everything? Beth couldn't shake her feeling of guilt, that she could have – should have – helped, nor for the fact that she'd found out the week before something that promised to change her life completely.

It had taken her a while to accept that it was good news, the fact that she was pregnant. It hadn't been planned and, whilst she and Rob had been seeing one another for two years and were very much in love, it wasn't a topic that dominated their conversations. But the decision had been taken out of their hands by a weird union of fate and a split condom.

Her awful sense of loss over Kathy was therefore tempered by the fact that she was going to be a mother. It was a wonderful feeling but it also filled her with fear, about what she was going to do, how it would affect her and Rob, how they would manage and what kind of mother she would make.

Sometimes, mixed with the news from Paris, those thoughts made her maudlin, the kind of thoughts for rainy nights when she was lying in bed alone, staring at the ceiling.

Right now, she knew what was going to happen. She was going to go home, finish packing and then tube it to Rob's, to spend the night there.

She smiled, wondering if he was looking forward to spending four days in Heyton yet.

Looking both ways – and invoking that particular prayer which Londoners use for crossing the road at rush-hour with taxis doing their best to become killing machines – Beth crossed Kingsway and walked towards Holborn tube station.

～

The usual mass of people thronged outside the station, individuals crammed against neighbours they would never be interested in talking to. They jostled for space and moaned about how the underground was getting worse, how the annoying bloody tourists always seemed to be carrying holdalls that were bigger than they were and how the people who reached past your face to hold on to the grip bars never seemed to wash or know what deodorant was.

Beth sidestepped the Big Issue seller, dug her travel card out of her wallet and joined what looked like the shortest queue for the ticket machines. Of course, it wasn't but she was soon through, the machine reading and then spitting her card out.

Generally, except on Fridays when there seemed to be twice as many commuters as usual, Beth liked the underground. She enjoyed the incongruity of the vast spaces, the escalators looking down like some kind of cathedral in reverse and the curved wall walkways, with their myriad posters for things that she would never see. The platforms, long and cramped, the carbon blackness below rails which themselves shined as bright as new. Some commuters clamoured for position, those who knew they'd get on at some time sitting on the benches, whilst others buying chocolate to tide them over until they got home.

Beth fell into step behind a short business-woman whose hair was shaved almost to her scalp, waiting to get onto the escalator.

And then she saw Kathy.

Her cousin was on the next escalator over, half a dozen steps from the top, her long blonde hair plaited neatly and resting down the back of her Armani coat. Her face, looking down, wasn't completely visible but Beth knew her well enough to see that it was her.

She felt the hairs on her arms stand on end.

Kathy was going down the escalator at Holborn tube station. Even though Beth knew that, at the moment, she was resting peacefully in the Pere La Chase cemetery in Paris.

"Excuse me," she said, brushing by the skinhead businesswoman.

"We're all in rush," said the woman grumpily.

"Sorry," Beth said quickly and, using the left side of the escalator, worked her way down until she was about level with Kathy. Except that it couldn't be Kathy, that was just silly.

Slotting herself between two Chinese businessmen, Beth leaned on the rail and said, "Hello? Kathy?"

Kathy turned and smiled, as solid a presence as a real person. "My God, Beth. Fancy seeing you here."

Beth blinked and looked up at the Chinese man standing above her. Curtly, he smiled at her and then looked away.

Beth looked back at Kathy, who'd started to work her way down the escalator. "Wait," she called and began to move down the escalator herself.

Her path was blocked by an elderly Japanese man, dressed in a bright yellow anorak, his short wife standing on the right with her eyes closed.

"Excuse me," she said, "I have to get past."

The Japanese man turned to her, uncomprehending. He pursed his lips and shook his head.

"Down," said Beth, making walking movements with her fingers. "I need to get down quickly."

The Japanese man, his eyes wide and watery, shook his head again.

"Bollocks," she said and leaned back on the right handrail, keeping an eye on Kathy. She was almost at the bottom now.

Beth willed her escalator to go faster, knowing that it was useless. Worse, the Japanese couple would probably leave it to the last minute to get off at the bottom, still two abreast and hold everyone up. Why pick now, rush hour, to come on the tube? Why not go on it an hour earlier?

Kathy reached the bottom, stepped off and out of the way of her fellow passengers. She looked up, waved to Beth and then walked away, disappearing into a tunnel.

"Come on," hissed Beth, the bottom of the escalator a few metres away yet. The old Japanese man appeared to be getting jittery and was stepping from foot to foot, his wife looking at him suspiciously. Beth watched his movements and realised that was her chance.

She stepped to her left, waited for the old man to put his weight on his right foot and then pushed past him, pressing her hands against his arm and she was by him.

The metal steps in front were almost empty and she took them a couple at a time, stood still until she was past the grille at the base so that her momentum didn't throw her into the opposite wall and then she was onto the tiled floor and after Kathy.

She moved as quickly as she could, sidestepping some people and pushing past others, ignoring their muttered curses.

She rounded a corner and stopped at a crossroads – which way? The Central Line, taking her to Tottenham Court Road and the Northern Line back to her little flat or the Piccadilly Line, into the heart of London or out to Cockfosters? She looked around quickly and just caught sight of a mane of golden hair moving around a corner ahead.

Piccadilly.

She ran down the corridor, shouting for Kathy, ignoring the strange looks that people were giving her.

The corridor ended, a platform each side of her. Into the city or out? Central London, she decided and ran down that passage and onto the platform, crowded with people.

She stood on tiptoe, stretching past her five foot eight, but couldn't see Kathy at all. Beth decided that she'd head for the front of the train and began to push her way past the waiting commuters. It was hot down here, damp and sticky and she could feel the sweat spring up onto her brow.

Forward, keep going. Stop, stand on tiptoes, see what can be seen.

There. A woman with long blonde hair.

Beth pushed forward, reached the woman but even as she put her hand on the dark jacketed shoulder, she knew she was wrong.

The woman, her features hard and aged, turned around and scowled at Beth. She apologised and the woman let out a torrent of abuse, in a language that Beth didn't understand.

"I'm sorry," she said again and pushed past the woman. She was close to the end of the platform now and about to turn around and push her way back to the other end, when she saw Kathy.

"Kathy!" she called, standing on tiptoes.

Her cousin turned, waved and shook her head.

Beth kept going, pushing past bodies until she was at the end of the platform, Kathy standing in front of her.

"You don't want to see this," she said.

"Kathy, no, stay and talk."

"Sorry, Bethy, I've got to go."

Beth felt a welcome breeze on her face and realised that the train was coming. Kathy stepped backwards, with carefully measured paces and pressed her fingers against the tiled walls. Beth watched her, knowing what she was going to do, but unable to move.

The train, still in the tunnel, sounded its horn and Beth reached for Kathy.

"No," she said, but the word was carried away by the sounds of brakes in the tunnel.

Kathy pushed away from the wall and ran, passing the yellow line and then she was jumping, suspended in the air like a shape on a child's mobile.

The train came out of the tunnel and Kathy hit squarely in the middle of the cab windows. Beth wondered if she'd caught the driver's compartment on the Metro train, if he'd had a chance to do anything as he saw the shape of the woman coming towards him. Did the sound of her body impacting still haunt his dreams?

Kathy was gone.

The train slowed to a stop and the doors opened, the platform emptying as the commuters forced themselves into carriages that weren't designed to hold quite so many people.

Beth found a bench and sat down as everything suddenly seemed to get on top of her and press down.

As the train pulled away, she put her head in her hands and began to cry.

CHAPTER 2

ROB WARREN LEANED BACK in his chair and glanced out of the narrow window that looked down onto the bustle of Holloway Road.

People were heading home, heedlessly crossing the road and ignoring the blare of horns and the cyclists, who seemed intent to take out as many pedestrians as they possibly could. He sighed and looked at his monitor. According to his PC clock, which ran slightly fast, it was five forty-one, leaving him another nineteen minutes to pretend that he was looking forward to going away.

Not that he wasn't, exactly. He and Beth would be together, it was free, and according to the weather reports it was going to be a gorgeous weekend. So it wouldn't be that bad. But a long weekend in Heyton? How the board must have pissed themselves laughing when they came up with that.

He looked at the workstation next to him, as empty as it had been all week. Michael was in Barbados with his girlfriend, probably right now ogling the topless lovelies as they sauntered around the pool.

It was, his colleagues told him, an annual treat at Dorset Travel – everyone was given a free ticket by the management team who drew locations and put tickets against each one.

"It's like watching the draw for the FA Cup," Michael had told him one lunchtime as they sat in the pub, drinking their lunch as the pre-packaged lasagnes in front of them cooled and solidified. "Twenty of us and ten locations, so they're pretty good odds and some of the holidays are excellent."

It was Michael's ticket that had turned out to be excellent – ten days in Barbados. Rob had watched the rest of the draw, pleased for Michael but wondering if his ticket was going to come through. With all the hassle this year and the lack of money, they hadn't planned to go on holiday and he would have loved to have taken Beth away. The holiday of a lifetime, perhaps?

"This is for the long weekend in Heyton," said Brian, his line manager and most of the analysts groaned. "And it's linked with ticket fourteen. Who has that?"

Rob knew he had it, without checking. It was Michael who looked over, saw it and raised Rob's hand. "Over here," he said and the rest of the analysts cheered. The only UK-based holiday, for the shortest period of time, in some rotten way it made sense to give it to the new guy. The next nearest to the mainland was the Isle of Wight, for Cowes week. Even the non-sailors in the office, which was everybody, wouldn't have minded that.

Beth had been excited when he told her that night, sitting across from one another in Pizza Hut.

"But we could have gone to Barbados," moaned Rob.

"Yes," said Beth brightly, "but even so. We're getting a free holiday and Heyton's not that bad a place."

Rob could remember childhood holidays there, as well as a couple he'd taken later with his best friend, and knew that she was right. It was just that it wasn't what he'd been hoping for.

"I know," he said, fully aware that he would come across as a whining shit, "but it could have been Barbados."

"Maybe next year."

"With Junior in tow?"

Beth nodded. "With Junior in tow. Now, are you going to eat that bit of garlic bread?"

Whatever happened, he would try to make the weekend a good one. He'd enjoy himself and make sure that Beth did too. As a plus, if the weather was as good as the reports were promising, they might even get plenty of sun.

At six o'clock, Rob shut his PC off, put his suit coat on and went out of the building with his colleagues, most of them taking the piss about how he was going to come home with food poisoning and his lower legs forever dyed shitty brown if he decided to paddle in the sea.

~

Beth caught the next train, found a seat in the last carriage and took her paperback out of her satchel. She skimmed the words on the page but none of them made sense – they could have been written in the same language as the one the woman had used to shout abuse at her before. The woman she'd thought was Kathy.

Why think of her now? Was this guilt or something else?

The mechanics of seeing her didn't bother Beth quite so much. She wasn't psychic, couldn't read palms or tea-leaves or tarot cards – she couldn't even pick the correct lottery numbers. But for a long time, she'd been able to see or feel things that didn't make any kind of rational sense. After a while, she began to call these occurrences her 'psychic episodes' and made a bit of joke about them.

The first had happened in her early teens and she now believed it coincided with the onset of her periods. It hadn't even seemed out of the ordinary at the time. She was in the garden shed, using her brother's chemistry set to conduct an experiment for homework, when she became aware of someone standing behind her. Assuming it was her brother and thinking that he was going to try and mess up what she was doing, as he invariably attempted every time, she told him to go away.

That's not nice, Lizzie.

It was her Granddad's voice. Her breath caught in her throat and her fingers tingled. He'd been dead three years.

When she turned around, he was standing by the door, leaning on the jamb with the same easy smile that she remembered, wearing a little pork-pie hat with a fishing lure stuck into the headband.

You okay?

"I'm fine, Granddad, how're you?"

Not quite feeling myself, he'd said, his easy smile not wavering. *I've got to go now, I just called by to say hello. You take care of yourself, won't you?*

"I will. Love you, Granddad."

Love you too. Look after your mum and dad and brother for me.

Then he was gone and her brother came in ten minutes later and turned the burner up too high and cracked the test tube. She didn't tell him, or her mum and dad, about Granddad.

Normally, what she saw were things or people she knew about, vague successions of images like a flickering old film, in situations that she could never have witnessed, shown to her as if she were a bystander to the drama.

Today, though, had been the worst. She could still feel it, the fear coursing through her veins and she could hear it in her ragged breathing. So why now?

It had to be because of everything that was playing on her mind, all of the things that she was trying to process – obviously without success. The pregnancy and how it would impact on her life, finding out about Kathy – perhaps the extra hormones she had now had linked with her grief and guilt

17

to create a lovely little interactive film where she got to watch her cousin kill herself.

Thanks, she thought. Thanks a lot.

The train stopped at Tottenham Court Road and she changed to the Northern Line north platform. She kept a wary eye out for Kathy, but didn't see her. The train arrived and she got on, heading for home.

~

Rob crossed the street, his coat over his shoulder, his sleeves rolled up and tie pulled down, looking like everyone else who'd come out of an air-conditioned office into the heat. The summer had been unusually warm and in his office alone, he'd heard of three burglaries, where people had gone to sleep with the window open a crack to try and let some air in. Fresh air did come in, but so did the neighbourhood dickheads, who made off with stereos, videos and DVD players.

He thought about Beth and wondered how she was doing.

It was still hard to believe that he was going to be a dad. He was a twenty-nine year old analyst who had worked and studied hard, to be kicked out of a job he loved because some idiot further up the food chain hadn't done his sums right; who lived in a flat that he'd begun to rent when his salary was through the roof and which he was now coming to realise would be a major millstone around his neck when the baby turned up.

He was the first of his circle of friends to be going through the fatherhood process. When Beth had told him, he hadn't quite known what to say or do – after all, it was hardly something that you got instructions for and it hadn't been the follow-on article to the salary survey he'd read in *FHM*.

~

It was a Friday night, what they called 'treat night' since the money got tighter. The Pizza Hut on the high street, where he'd told her afterwards about going to Heyton, in their usual spot by the window.

He'd known something was wrong. Beth hadn't been her normal self all evening and he was trying to figure out if he'd put his foot in it when she came out with her announcement.

"Rob," she said, "you know I love you."

"I love you too," he'd said, automatically.

She paused and he looked up. "I've got something to tell you."

Smiling, he took a sip of his lager. "Okay."

Her smile was slow and shy. "You might want to put your drink down."

"Why?"

She breathed in deeply, rested her hands on the tabletop and leaned back. "Because I'm pregnant."

"What?" Later, as he replayed the conversation in his head, he was so glad that he'd managed to bite back the urge to say 'you're joking', as if it was the kind of thing that normal, rational people would joke about on a 'treat night'.

Beth leaned forward, her smile fading slowly. "I'm pregnant. I did the test this morning. One of those new digital kits, supposed to be very accurate."

Now Rob leaned back. "Bloody hell," he said, his mind racing. Pregnant – he was going to be a father. What would happen? Where would they go? He could hardly afford his flat and hers was barely big enough for the pair of them, let alone two adults and a little person.

Beth let the silence run for a few moments and then said, "Are you pissed off with me?"

He looked at her then, properly and realised that her eyes were gleaming with tears. "What? No, of course I'm not, I'm just…"

"Thinking about what we're going to do?"

"Yes," he said, nodding, "that kind of thing."

"I want to keep it."

She said it with such definite finality that he didn't even bother to question it, not that it had occurred to him before she said it. "Well yes, of course. I mean, we're going to have to figure some stuff out, but absolutely."

"So you're okay with it?"

"Well, it's a shock," he said and ran a hand through his hair, thinking, I'm going to be a dad. "But we used condoms."

She pursed her lips. "You remember that one that split?"

He looked out of the window. "I do. Shit, I thought we got everything."

"It only needs a bit, Rob."

"I know, I know." He took a deep breath, vaguely aware that the rest of Pizza Hut – the rest of London and the known world – seemed to have dropped away from around him, leaving just him and the woman he loved sitting across from each other with this piece of news floating above the table. His mind flashed a hundred or more images, none of them substantial enough for him to grasp. Until he realised that Beth was looking at him, the tears still there.

"Well," he said and cleared his throat, nodding, "I think this is fairly cool, you know?"

"Really?" Beth's face lit up with a big smile and she leaned over the table, balancing on her elbows and gave him a big, noisy kiss on the lips.

"Thank you, Rob."

"What for?"

"For being you."

~

Rob reached the tube station, fed his card through and went down the escalators. Since they were going away tomorrow, they'd decided that tonight would be treat night and Beth would stay at his.

He liked it when she did. He enjoyed living alone, but having her around often made him feel stupidly happy. He didn't mind, as so many of his friends and colleagues seemed to, the fact that she took up more of the bathroom than he did, even though she only normally stayed for the weekend. He liked that he could smell her around the place, he liked to wake up with her in bed beside him and he loved to fall asleep with her cuddled up in his arms.

After the initial joy at the news – and having told their parents who seemed keen, but reserved – the logistical problems hit Rob with a wallop. What would they do for money? Where would they live? After a while, it became obvious – they could live in his flat and fit in most of the accoutrements that a new-born would require but it would mean Beth giving up her flat and moving in with him, full-time.

He liked the idea and it made sense, but it also meant that they would be making much more of a commitment beyond habitation and finances. He was certain that Beth was the one for him, but did she feel the same way?

So he'd decided that the Heyton weekend would be the ideal time to ask her to move in with him. After all, what was the worst that could happen?

CHAPTER 3

BY THE TIME BETH unlocked the front door of the house, she felt hot and sweaty and uncomfortable. She knew a shower would sort her out, but didn't have the time for it.

She closed the door, sorted through her post on the table against the wall and went up the stairs slowly and quietly, so as not to disturb her landlord who would come out, in his vest and tight shorts, to make sure that she was okay.

Beth unlocked and pushed open the door of her flat, the heat pressing back at her. Once in, she backheeled the door shut and dropped her keys on top of the small bookcase in the hall.

She'd arranged to be at Rob's by seven thirty and was pleased to be staying over. She'd talked him out of leaving at eight o'clock, reasoning that spending so long parked on the M25 in an un-air-conditioned car wouldn't make the moods of either of them the most desirable to go on holiday with. He'd finally acquiesced, but wanted to be away by ten.

She opened the kitchen window, closing her eyes against the light breeze that brushed her face. It wasn't cool, but it was better than the ambient air in her flat.

Beth liked to stand at the window when she got home from work, looking out at the world as she waited for the kettle to boil. As views went it wasn't wonderful, but she enjoyed watching the bits and pieces of the lives she could see in the houses that backed onto hers.

But there wasn't time for that tonight. She clicked the kettle on and went into the bedroom to pack.

"Hot or cold," she asked her reflection. The reports she'd seen reckoned the weather on the east coast would be very warm so she packed both of her bikinis and a jumper as well, in case they decided to wander along the beach one evening.

By the time the kettle had boiled, she was packed and sat in the lounge watching the end of the local news whilst she drank her coffee.

~

Beth left the house, after checking a few times that she'd switched everything off that should be switched off, and that the jade tree her sister-in-law had given her was fully watered at seven twenty. She thought her tardiness was one of her endearing character quirks, though she knew that not many other people necessarily shared that point of view.

Her stuff for the weekend, crammed into a rucksack and slung over one shoulder, was heavier than she'd thought and she'd put both arms through the straps before she'd even gotten to the end of her road. Her handbag ended up on her front, bumping gently against her with each step.

Absently, she rubbed her belly though she knew there was pretty much nothing to feel. According to the Miriam Stoppard book Rob had bought her the day after she'd told him the news, Junior was currently the size of a small strawberry. That didn't mean a lot – she'd seen some tiny strawberries so she had no point of reference. But its heart and internal organs were established so she rubbed her belly every now and then, to let Junior know she was thinking of him.

Most of the time, it still didn't seem real. One of her friends from school – they still met up whenever she went back to Gaffney to see her parents – was on her fourth and had been very excited that Beth was now 'in the family way'. But even her enthusiasm didn't match what Beth felt, that she and Rob had created another life and it was growing even now, sometimes causing her to throw up in the mornings, but otherwise just hanging around waiting for the gestation process to kick in properly.

She was going to be a mum and it was going to take a lot of getting used too.

She reached the tube station just as the train pulled in and got on. There were three people in her carriage, a harassed looking woman barking orders into a mobile, an old man staring into middle distance and a teenager, drumming on his legs to a tinny beat that Beth could hear through his headphones. She took her paperback out of her rucksack, flicked to her page and began to read.

~

Rob's intercom buzzed at eight, making him jump and he got up to answer it, surprised that Beth was so early.

"Yes?"

"Food delivery," said a very nasal voice, "for Miztuh Warren."

He smiled. Beth hadn't pinched her nose to get a stupid voice for a while now. "I'll buzz the door."

"You wanta tha free Coke wiz zit?"

He laughed. "Yes and the gorgeous woman that I get because it's a late delivery."

"I have her in-a zee car, she make a lot of zee noise. I have-a to-a tape-a her mouth shut."

"Sounds like a good idea," he said and pressed the button. He put his front door on the latch and went out onto the landing, listening as Beth made her way up the stairs.

Finally, her head appeared and he smiled. "Hey, you forgot the grub."

She waved her hand at him. "Ah, he left it on the doorstep."

He met her at the top of her stairs and they hugged.

"So how's my favourite girl today?" he said, kissing her.

"Doing okay."

"And Junior?" he asked, gently rubbing her belly.

"Doing okay," she said and kissed him, letting her rucksack slide off her shoulder. "So what are we having tonight?"

Rob picked up her rucksack and led her into the flat. "I thought we could try out the new Indian on Turner Street, so long as the spice doesn't give you heartburn or anything."

She stroked his cheek. "I get heartburn from Indian's at the best of times, so I imagine it will."

He put his wallet in his pocket, locked the door and they went down the stairs, hand in hand.

~

The Curry House on Turner Street was as good as he'd heard it would be and they each went for the three-course option, staggering home with groaning bellies.

When they got in, Rob opened the windows and put the kettle on whilst Beth went for a shower. When she was out, a towel wrapped around her and drinking her coffee, he went for a shower.

Finished, they sat on the sofa, he against an arm, Beth lying with her head in his lap. He twirled his fingers through her hair idly, enjoying the sensation of peace.

"Are you happy?" she said, after a while.

"Yes," he said, surprised as he thought she'd fallen asleep. "You're here, so why wouldn't I be?"

"Are you looking forward to the weekend?"

"I am, but I would be even more if we were going to Barbados."

"When does Michael come back?"

"Next Thursday."

She tilted her head back so that she was looking at him and he was surprised by the wave of love that washed over him. He thought she was beautiful, knew that he loved her, but sometimes it seemed as if he was looking at her afresh, for the first time. Such as now – he was suddenly aware of both how gorgeous she was and how lucky he was that she was lying on his sofa, in one of his towels. When she smiled, as she was doing now, it brightened up her whole face and made her eyes shine.

"Well you can compare tans then, can't you?"

"I thought I could maybe just swim in the sea, then not bother to wash all the crap off."

"It's not going to be that bad. You're exaggerating now."

"Do you intend to go in the sea?"

She stuck her lower lip out, as if deep in thought. "I might paddle, but I think I'll leave the actual swimming to the pool."

"The hotel won't be that grand, you know."

"Well there's a municipal pool isn't there? On the front, just down from the Sea-Life centre."

"Do you think it'll be safe?" he said, trying to look serious.

She blew out her breath. "I've never known anyone who was so ungrateful to get a free holiday. It's going to be fun, Rob Warren," she said mock-sternly, "you just wait and see."

~

Later, with Rob sleeping deeply behind her, his arm over her side and his hand resting across her belly, Beth looked through the gap that he'd left between the curtains, to let some air in. The sky was clear, stars twinkling above the glow of light pollution.

"I love you," she said quietly.

He mumbled something in reply and shifted position slightly, his hand dropping onto the mattress.

Suddenly, she wanted his hand back. She wanted to turn over, to wake him up and find out what his plans for the future were. Something was on his mind, she could see that, but apart from cursory conversations since she'd told him the news in Pizza Hut, nothing had been decided or even discussed with any real seriousness. She loved him, but what about his feelings? He said he loved her, told her that he wanted to be a father, but how much of that was front, if any of it? Would he tell her the truth now or wait until later on in the pregnancy when she was fat and ungainly, a whale compared to other women on the street and in his office? Or would everything turn out just right, as it often did in books and films, the ones that made both of them groan at how unrealistic and unlikely they were?

Beth felt a tear run down her cheek and soak into the pillow.

"What's going to happen?" she said to the moon.

"Go to Heyton," said Rob groggily.

She smiled, wiped away a fresh tear and closed her eyes, clutching Rob's arm tightly.

CHAPTER 4

HEYTON, ON THE EAST coast a few miles from Lowestoft, had grown over the years into a thriving holiday resort. It was popular with a broad cross-section of people, with the town centre on the western side, adjacent to the river Heyt and the seaside attractions on Marine Road, which ran for a mile along the seafront and ended in a residential area and some warehousing.

The north end of Marine Road was the oldest, with a theatre complex and ornate pier, both of which had been sturdily built a century before but were now showing signs of neglect. The theatre had once showcased some of the greatest names in British entertainment but now housed an arcade, restaurant, shops and the town's 'first-run' cinema. The pier had suffered similar ignominy and now played host to various stalls and stands and a small variety theatre that scrabbled for bookings.

On the town side of Marine Road as it runs south, there are restaurants and hotels, arcades and pubs and shops that only cater for the holidaymaker. The Heyton Empire, on the corner of Duncan Hill, had tried to retain its splendour but it was fading now, a gothic building that showed old films and doubled up as an occasional Bingo hall.

On the seafront side of Marine Road is The Royalty – a theatre that specialises in bawdy plays – a Sea-Life centre and municipal pool, crazy golf courses, souvenir shacks that spring up each summer as if from nowhere (and are never the same twice) and the funfair.

The Fair began in 1903 with a Helter Skelter, a fortune-teller and a coconut shy and grew with the town. Now it contained what most other seaside fairgrounds did – shooting galleries, Hook-A-Duck and the like – in addition to some thrill rides, like The Waltzer, Ghost Train, Dodgems, High Roller, the Log Flume and kiddie rides. Its huge wooden rollercoaster attracts interest from aficionados but leaves those accustomed to the sensations of rides like the Nemesis and The Big One completely nonplussed.

Behind the Fair is a pocket park, known locally as The Yard, formed from a strip of land deemed unsuitable for building on. Its centrepiece is a memorial, a six-foot granite spike that originally celebrated the lives of sailors lost in the Wash. During the summer, The Yard is used by picnicking families who don't want to get sand in their sandwiches whilst in the close season, it's the hang-out of teens, who want to be well away from the main drag of town to indulge in their passions – drinking plenty of White Lightning, taking drugs and trying to collect more lovebites than their mates.

Needless to say, quite a few children in Heyton have been conceived in The Yard.

Separating The Yard from the first of three warehouses is a narrow road that allows beach access for safety vehicles. After the warehouses, holiday homes line the road to the inlet of the Heyt.

As with any coastal town dependant on tourist income, Heyton suffered with the advent of package holidays and, as the recession bit, the nature of the businesses in town changed – the smaller, family-run shops closed down and even some of the High Street stores moved out. Pound shops began to proliferate along Commerce Street, which linked Marine Road with the town centre. These competed for business with trinket shops, T-shirt printing shops and joke stores. The waxworks, once a proud attraction, was much reduced in glory, the lesser income meaning that it couldn't afford to upgrade its dummies. Most children hadn't even been thought about when Daley Thompson – the last but one addition – was claiming his glory. A concession to modernity was made with a model of David Beckham, which everyone agreed looked nothing like the man.

Lately, the biggest concern for the town council was the state of the beach embankment. Years of erosion had gnawed away at it, putting the future of everything on the shore side of Marine Road in doubt. Taking a cue from Morecombe Bay, the council voted to strengthen the weaker parts with large rocks.

A local university produced a report, which explained what would happen to the town if these defences weren't put in. Their doom and gloom predictions had the desired effect and the coastal defences were budgeted in, the leader of the council taking the case personally to the local MP.

The work was planned to start at The Yard and move down the beach to the Sea-Life centre. In addition, it was hoped that the rocks would provide a fertile ground for crustacean life, which would enable the council to upgrade The Yard, since it could be classed as an educational capital project.

The coastal defences project started in June.

At ten past six on Friday morning, Heyton was covered by a thin mist and the sun glowed white through it.

Steve Ellis wasn't paying much attention to either – he had to be on the beach by six and he was currently driving down Commerce Street in his JCB, fighting a pointless battle with his watch – and his temper was already fraying. He'd been up most of the night – his wife, Donna and son, Josh, both had a bug, which was making the boy repeatedly sick – and all he wanted was some sleep.

He was at least grateful that his son was there for him to worry about, unlike the poor sods whose boy had gone missing on Wednesday. That was the one thing Steve hated about living in Heyton, the bad things that happened, made worse because the victims were here trying to enjoy themselves.

Missing children were almost a fact of life at the seaside, the occurrence rate seeming to grow year on year. The majority of them weren't snatched by perverts or the like, they simply wandered off in search of adventure and excitement and were often found either drowned or caught up in machinery in various places, all of them dead. By his reckoning, for every ten children that went missing, seven or eight would never been seen alive again.

He couldn't comprehend the pain the parents must be going through. Josh often bugged the shit out of him, but Steve didn't think he could go back to living a normal life if anything were to happen to his son. He'd helped out with the initial search yesterday and had checked through the Fair with two dozen other people, but they'd found nothing.

Toby, the missing boy, was seven and the pictures his parents had given to the local paper showed a blond haired kid with freckles, a dimpled grin, a couple of missing teeth and an innocent brightness in his eyes that must have been difficult not to think about as they tried to sleep.

At the end of Commerce Street, Steve checked that nothing was coming and turned right into Marine Road, the mist thinning now and curling around lamp-posts and benches. With the road empty, he put his foot down, willing the JCB to go faster, hoping that by only being a little bit late, his site foreman, Chris Valentine, wouldn't give him too much hell.

He passed the ill-named Excelsior hotel and not for the first time, thought it looked like a giant dick pointing at the sky.

His frustration at the JCB's lack of pace exacerbated the fatigue worrying at his temples, which was making his eyes feel prickly. His shoulders felt knotted and his temper was balancing on a knife edge – he knew that if someone said the wrong thing to him today, he would explode. He glanced at his watch again quickly, saw that it was now twelve minutes past six and swore at it.

The JCB cut through a wedge of mist, wisps curling into his cab and brushing past his face. It made him cough and stung his eyes more.

"For fuck's sake," he shouted and stamped his foot on the accelerator, but it made no difference. The JCB was going as fast as it possibly could.

Then, to his relief, the Log Flume seemed to materialise out of the gloom. A few yards later and the mist lifted, as if by magic and he could see the Fair and the warehouse behind it. Not far now and if he could shave a bit of time off, rather than go through the rigmarole of swiping his card to get onto the beach access road, he might not be in too much trouble.

It would mean cutting through The Yard, but a lot of people did it and the ground was as hard as rock after the summer they'd had, so it wasn't like he'd churn it up with the JCB's massive wheels.

He smiled. The shortcut might save him three or four minutes and if Valentine was further down the beach supervising the offloading of more boulders, he might even get away with being late.

Still at top speed, he chugged past the Log Flume and the slatted fence of the Fair, the highest peaks of the rollercoaster visible against the clear blue sky.

He liked the rollercoaster. His and Donna's first date had been a night at the fair and he'd persuaded her to go on the rollercoaster with him. She didn't really want to, but he cajoled her until she agreed and once they'd set off, he could see that she was clearly terrified. Where he'd spent ages wondering how he could get his arm around her, she clung to him from the start to the finish and he didn't have to do any work.

Smiling, he looked back at the road. The corner of the Fair was close, where it joined The Yard.

He checked his mirrors, saw there was no-one else around and turned the steering wheel hard.

The JCB bounced up the kerb, jolting him in his seat and he had to grip the wheel hard to avoid having it spin out of control.

He yanked it around, felt the back end slide slightly and then he was on the grass. He steered a diagonal course across The Yard, so that he would bypass the memorial which stood in the centre, the spike of it sitting in a bed of marble, with stone-work leading out from that as the lives it remembered had increased from the original sailors it was intended for, to the men the town had lost in the two World Wars. Against these stones, circling the memorial, were eight small pillars, with a chain hung between them.

One of the front wheels caught in something, jarring and spinning the steering wheel out of his grip. He swore at it and tried to grab hold as the wheel righted itself, throwing the JCB to the left and jolting him out of his seat and into the window. He sat back with a thud, the damage done – the steering wheel was turning of its own accord, the uneven ground dictating the route.

He wrestled with the steering wheel, turning it to his right but it didn't move immediately. He felt sweat running down his back and forehead, into his already sore eyes and stamped on the brakes.

The wheels locked and he realised with horror that he was going to hit the memorial. He took his foot off the brake and they freed, giving him some control. He jerked the wheel right again but it was too late.

Dimly, through the juddering sound of the engine that filled the cab, he heard something crunch and snap under the wheels.

"Fuck." He kept the wheel turned to the right and braked again, as the bucket glanced past the spike without touching it. For that, at least, he could be grateful.

The JCB came to a shuddering halt and he leaned his head on the wheel, breathing deeply.

"Shit, shit, shit."

His head was thumping and he felt sick, not willing to believe that he'd managed to damage the memorial. It had been there for years, surviving everything that nature and the towns youth could throw at it; it was the focal point of the November 11th Memorial services and now, to try and save a few minutes, he'd damaged it.

He got out of the cab on unsteady legs and leaned against the tyre, waiting for the nausea to pass, staring at the ground and breathing deeply. He rubbed his face and looked up.

The memorial was still standing. One of the small pillars had been knocked over and the chain that it supported had snapped and was lying on the ground like an unwound length of garden hose. Somehow, he'd missed the next pillar along, though he didn't know how.

Not too bad, he thought. If he could stand the pillar up, he might be able to fix it to its supporting rod and get away with it. The chain link might have snapped, but he could sort that without too much hassle. If he remembered rightly from his youth, it wasn't the best quality chain in the whole world and it was regularly snapped by people trying to walk the tightrope on it. As he himself had once done.

He walked over to the memorial, glancing around to see if anyone had seen his act of vandalism, but he still seemed to be on his own.

The in-memorium stones that he'd run over seemed to be okay, without any visible cracks on them and he knelt by the pillar. The tyre had obviously gone over one side of it and pushed it off the support rod. He picked up the masonry, surprised at how light it was and checked it for damage. It looked as if its light weight had actually helped to save it and he slotted the gap side onto the rod. It stayed.

Steve looked up to the sky, to thank whoever it was who was looking over him this morning and pulled the broken chain to him. Again, he was in luck. One of the links had literally popped apart from its neighbour and he rethreaded it.

Satisfied, he stepped back and breathed a sigh of relief, staring at the memorial. There didn't seem to be any real sign that he'd almost driven into it.

Until he saw the crack.

"Oh shit," he said and stepped over the chain and the stones and knelt in front of the spike, looking at the ragged crack that ran across the marble base from the edge of one of the stones almost to the spike itself.

This couldn't be happening. If need be, he could come back tonight after dark and fix the pillar and nobody need be any the wiser but marble? How was he going to repair that?

He leaned forward, running his fingers gently across the crack. It was deep, the marble had separated by an inch or so in places and, as he leaned further, he became aware of a low buzzing sound. It wasn't like the buzzing sound of a fly or wasp, but something deeper and heavier, like machinery was running underground.

His fingers explored more of the crack and he became aware that he could feel vibrations through them, which got more pronounced as the buzzing sound got louder.

"Shit, what have I done?"

The vibrations were running through his whole hand now and he heard the links of his wristwatch clicking together.

This can't have been his fault? What could he have done to make the marble vibrate?

It didn't make sense. Nor did the pale green smoke that now seeped out of the crack, where it almost touched the spike.

"What the fuck?" he said quietly, his heart thumping painfully in his chest. Was something toxic buried under there? If it was, what would happen if he breathed any of it in?

Quickly, he pushed himself up into a squat and pulled his handkerchief out of his pocket, holding it over his nose and mouth. It wasn't a perfect defence, but it was better than nothing.

The buzzing had stopped and he looked around. Perhaps it had been some kind of insect after all, though he didn't think so. Or perhaps…

Something brushed his face and his thudding heart seemed to miss a beat, then another. His throat felt like it was burning and he dragged in a ragged breath, not quite believing what he was looking at, his eyes stinging more now than they had when the mist had gone in them on Marine Road.

The smoke swirled and thickened in front of his face, seeming to move of its own volition rather than with the air currents, but through it he could see a female face.

The woman's face was long, framed by wild hair. Her jawline was strong, her lips thin and pursed, her cheekbones high.

Steve pushed back, skidding along the grass on his behind to try and get away from whatever it was he was looking at.

CONJURE

The face followed him, the cheeks moving slightly as if they were drawing breath. He was convinced that it wasn't the air moving them – as unreal as this was, as unreal as this had to be, the face was real. Or as real as it could be, seeing as how it was made of the smoke – green, with dark shadows at the hairline and under the cheekbones and around the eyes.

Perhaps he'd breathed some of that smoke in, perhaps all of this was a hallucination.

He stood up, the smoke face right in front of his and he could feel the breath coming through the woman's nose. The hair seemed to grow, until he realised that the smoke was gathering, showing him more of her. Her neck and shoulders, hair tumbling over them; more – her sternum and bare breasts, the nipples shadowed.

It's nothing to fear, he heard a woman say. The face had moved its lips, but how could she talk to him?

"Leave me alone, get away from me."

His head was spinning, like he was about to suffer the mother of all hangovers. Within a few moments it had cleared and he ran to the JCB, pulling open the door and climbing into the cab without looking behind him.

He switched the engine on, gripped the steering wheel and screamed. The woman was in front of him, entwined with the steering wheel.

It's nothing to fear, you might like it.

The buzzing sound came back, louder than before and he jammed his palms against his ears, but it didn't block the sound. The woman moved closer to him, puckering her lips as if she expected a kiss.

The buzzing set his teeth on edge and sharp pains dug into his temples.

"Leave me alone," he yelled and then the woman was gone and so was the buzzing. The pain in his temples flared twice, hard enough to make him wince, before subsiding to a level that was there, but tolerable.

Cautiously, he let go of his ears and looked around but couldn't see the woman. He leaned his head back, bringing several more spikes of pain and closed his eyes.

"Fucking hell," he said and only just had time to lean out of the cab door before the vomit came, spattering on the steps, wheel arch and grass.

More vomit, his throat and eyes burning. He dropped out of the cab and knelt on all fours on the grass.

He didn't believe he could vomit so much.

When he was finished he stared at the stinking pool of bile in front of him and began to retch. But it was done now, whatever it was. The pain in his head had subsided as well, reminding him of how a hangover would feel at lunchtime the next day.

He got to his feet and wiped his face on his T-shirt, his handkerchief missing somewhere. He thought it might be over by the memorial but he didn't want to go over there and search for it.

Why?

He frowned. There was something there, something in his mind, that told him not to go up to the memorial but he couldn't figure out what it was and didn't understand it. After all, he'd been coming to The Yard since he was a kid, nothing terrible could happen here.

Confusion gripped Steve – he couldn't comprehend any of this. Why the weird feeling, why was he standing over a pool of vomit that had to be his, why wasn't he in the JCB? He walked back to the machine, climbed in and slammed the door and steered the tractor onto the access road.

He glanced at his watch and saw that it was now six thirty. That didn't make any sense either, surely it hadn't taken him fifteen minutes to get from Marine Road to here?

He shrugged. If he was going to get into trouble with Chris Valentine, it might as well be for thirty minutes as fifteen.

"Who gives a shit anyway?" he muttered, as the JCB drove onto the sand.

CHAPTER 5

BETH COULD SMELL BLOSSOM and when she opened her eyes, the orchard spread out in front of her.

It seemed bigger and wider than she remembered it, from when she and Kathy had played there as children, riding from Kathy's on their bikes.

From behind a tree came a little girl with curly blonde hair, wearing jeans with sequins and a white T-shirt with Piglet on the front.

Beth stared, unable to believe that she was looking at her cousin as a child.

'Hello, Bethy,' said Kathy and she turned and ran into the trees.

Beth ran after her, heedless of the bracken and long grass, jumping easily over fallen logs.

Finally, Kathy stopped running and leaned against a tree, her face and eyes bright.

'How many shall we take?' she asked.

'How many of what?'

'These memories,' said Kathy, screwing her face up as if she thought Beth was the biggest idiot ever. 'We might not be able to come back here, so we want to get as many as we can.'

'Why won't we be able to come back?'

Kathy slid down the tree, until she was sitting at an odd angle on one of the roots. Her hair grew, straightening out and darkening slightly, past her shoulder and onto her T-shirt, where her breasts now pushed at the fabric, giving Piglet new contours on which to jump and frolic. Her face lengthened and thinned out, her legs growing until her jeans looked like shorts.

Her cousin was now an adult, her face sad and unhappy, her eyes full of tears. 'We can't always come back,' she said, 'I can see that now.'

'I don't understand.'

A dark line drew itself across Kathy's left cheek, up past her temple and across her forehead. Blood oozed from the line and trickled down her face, as her eyes clouded and rolled up.

'You can't get back,' she said.

Beth stared at her cousin's corpse and screamed.

~

"Beth?"

Beth opened her eyes slowly. Sunlight streamed through the gap in the curtains.

"Hey, gorgeous. I've made you a coffee. Did you sleep well?"

"Had a weird dream," she said and rubbed her eyes.

"A bad one?"

She tried to think about it, but the images didn't make any sense. "Can't remember."

Rob sat on the edge of the bed and stroked her cheek gently. "Don't worry about it then. If you do, you might remember."

He smiled and in that expression she could see how much he loved her and it warmed her. When she was younger, her mum had said that she knew Dad was the man for her when, on the second date, he'd looked at her in a certain way. Beth had never really understood what she meant and hadn't seen it with any of her previous boyfriends. But she understood now, in the way that Rob looked at her.

"I won't then," she said and felt a familiar lurch in her belly. "Oh shit."

"What's up?"

"I need the bathroom," she said and fought to free herself from the duvet, which had wrapped itself around her.

Rob got up as she jumped out of bed and ran for the bathroom. She knelt in front of the toilet, her hands on the cold porcelain and looked into the water, her own face rippling back at her.

Then she was sick.

By the time she was done, Rob was in the kitchen sipping a mug of tea. He put it down, a concerned look on his face and hugged her.

"Mmmm, that's nice," she said.

"You okay?"

"I'm fine now," she said and shrugged. "It comes and goes. Haven't had it all this week."

"One of the joys of pregnancy, eh?"

She laughed and picked up her coffee, which he'd brought through from the bedroom.

"Did you fancy having some breakfast?"

"I'd never turn my nose up at breakfast, you should know that by now."

~

Steve Ellis switched off the JCB engine and climbed out of the cab.

His lateness hadn't been noticed, so he'd got to work and waited until ten o'clock for his first break. He parked to the south of the warehouse so that he was on his own and sat on the sand, his back to the tyre, out of the glare of the sun.

The sea was calm, the sky clear blue with only the slightest hint of cloud – a perfect day. Steve wondered if Josh and Donna were up yet and how they were both feeling.

He felt rough. His head ached and his eyes stung, but he supposed both could be due to lack of sleep. His stomach, though, was unsettled and twice he'd been overcome by nausea and had to spit out foul-tasting wads of saliva.

Something nagged at him too, about this morning's journey and why he couldn't remember all of it. He remembered the rush, thinking about the missing child and cutting across The Yard, but then there was a gap, before he was on all fours with a pool of vomit in front of him.

So what had happened? Did he have Josh's sick bug? That would explain his stomach and the vomit, but not the lapse of memory.

He uncapped his flask and poured himself a coffee.

From high above, a seagull called to its mate and they swooped down to land a few feet in front of Steve, checking to see if there was any food to scavenge. There was, in the cab, a packed lunch that Donna had made up for him, but he couldn't face eating it now.

"Git," he said and waved his hands to shoo them away. They squawked, lifted into the air and circled a few times, before landing back on the sand and staring at him. "Go on, I haven't got any food."

The gulls moved closer, as he sipped his coffee and he kicked at the sand, showering them. They shook it off, squawking and then flew away.

Steve watched them go, then leaned his head against the tyre and closed his eyes.

The water is cold and rough hands are on his shoulders, chest and face, holding him under.

He opens his eyes, but the water is black and churned up by his exertions. He can't get the hands off and his lungs are starting to burn.

He kicks out but doesn't connect with anything, though he must have been close because the hands push him down further into the yielding surface he's pressed against. He opens his mouth, desperate to breathe and scream for help and foul tasting water rushes down his throat.

Steve jerked awake, spilling his coffee over his leg, breathing hard. He glanced around quickly, but nobody was near him and the sea was as calm as before.

He rubbed his face and watched the two seagulls land on the beach in front of him again.

~

They enjoyed a perfect greasy breakfast at the little café around the corner where Rob usually got his morning bacon butties. Feeling full and refreshed, they walked back to Rob's flat.

After she checked through her own rucksack to make certain she had everything, Beth scanned Ceefax for traffic and weather news whilst Rob did his last minute packing.

When he'd finished, they went downstairs and loaded their stuff into his Cavalier. He gave Beth a sheet of paper he'd been given at work, with instructions on how to get to the hotel.

"Do you think it'll take us long?" Beth asked.

"A good couple of hours, probably. The Clairmont isn't expecting us until two, so we've got plenty of time. We can stop for lunch perhaps, if we see a nice pub. Or there's bound to be a Little Chef or a McDonald's somewhere."

"Mmmm," said Beth, smiling and rubbing her belly, "greasy breakfast and then a Mickey D's. Ambassador, you are spoiling us."

Rob laughed, put the car into gear and pulled away from the kerb.

~

Steve climbed back into the JCB cab, feeling sick. He hadn't been able to finish his coffee and had thrown it at the gulls, who'd squawked their displeasure and flown away.

He stowed his flask under the seat and switched the engine on.

He's out of the water, being carried by half a dozen men. He can't understand how he didn't drown, but this is after as he can feel the water on his skin and where the wind blows against him, it's bitingly cold. He is hoisted over their heads, as if they're pallbearers carrying him to his own funeral.

He's carried to a patch of waste ground, where a hole has been dug and lined with stone. He knows that the hole is intended for him and he tries to kick himself free, but the pallbearers grips are so tight he can feel their fingers digging into his skin.

As the hole in the ground gets closer he screams.

His voice doesn't sound like his.

～

Since they'd left it until the rush hour had died down, they were out of London quickly. Within an hour, they were driving through the Fens, the roads stretching far into the distance until they were just a blur in the heat haze.

"I hate the Fens," grumbled Rob.

"Why?"

They were the last car in a convoy of six, behind a mini-bus full of old people. She could tell that he was getting impatient, tootling along at fifty miles an hour, but he wouldn't risk overtaking five other cars to get past them, however far ahead he could see.

"Because there's nothing here. This is the real road to hell, not the bloody M25."

"What do you mean? It's beautiful here."

He glanced at her, his expression suggesting that she was mad. "Beautiful? Which part?"

Beth laughed. "You're a city boy, that's your problem."

"Oh right," he said, laughing as well, "and Gaffney is a rural town?"

"It's surrounded by countryside."

"Yeah, but not countryside that you can see for miles over. Where are the hills, the winding roads? Where's the interest?"

"Philistine," she tutted, shaking her head. "What about the view?"

"What view? Some farmhouses, loads of fields that are all churned up and covered with shit and about a million electricity pylons."

"You have no poetry in your soul," said Beth.

"If I want poetry, I can go to a reading."

She laughed. "You've got to admit, the windmills are nice though."

The minibus slowed almost to a stop to negotiate a roundabout and Rob pulled the Cavalier up opposite a driveway. It was lined with hedges that blocked the bulk of the house behind them from view. All that could be seen was the black-tiled roof.

Behind the house, a white windmill stood in a field, its sails turning slowly.

"Bloody hell," said Rob, "look at that."

He was looking out of his window, so she leaned over to see. A telephone pole stood a hundred yards or so from the windmill, closer to the house and it took her a while to work out what was wrong with it.

A dozen crows were nailed to the thick wooden pole, some fresh with plump bellies and dark plumage. Others had been there for a long time and it appeared other birds had feasted on them.

"Jesus," she said.

"Wouldn't a scarecrow work better?" asked Rob slowly.

A brightly coloured ball came over the hedge and bounced into the driveway, close to the road. It wasn't fully inflated and the bounces died quickly, the ball rolling back down the slope. A small boy, wearing a Manchester United T-shirt and shorts, ran out from behind the hedge. He reached for his ball and shouted over his shoulder to someone Beth couldn't see.

He grabbed the ball with one hand, his fingers sinking into it and turned away.

"Oh," said Beth, with an involuntary gasp. Whatever she'd been expecting to see, it wasn't that the little boy would only have one full arm, his right ending in a puckered stump above where his elbow should have been. Swallowing, she looked back at the road, willing the minibus to move.

Rob put the car into gear, obviously as uncomfortable as she was. "Come on, come on," he said.

Presently, the minibus negotiated the roundabout and pulled away. The little boy had gone back behind the hedge, to continue his game.

They drove in silence for several miles, Beth's mind spinning, though she couldn't tell if it was the little boy and his disability or the crows that was bothering her most. Or was it that, back there, was a kind of existence that she couldn't begin to imagine?

The minibus was gone by then, down an unmarked side road and Rob was keeping the speed in the mid-sixties.

"I had another of my episodes yesterday," said Beth, looking out of the window at the vast flatness, feeling disconnected from her surroundings.

"Really? What happened?"

She looked at him. "I saw Kathy on the underground. She was going down the escalator next to me and I followed her onto the platform. She threw herself in front of a train."

"Christ, Beth, that's awful," Rob grimaced, "why didn't you say something before?"

"I don't know, it just didn't seem like the kind of thing to say."

"So what made you say it now? Was it that kid back there, or the crows?"

"I don't know."

"You should have said something last night. You know you can talk to me about these things."

She knew that he meant it, but she also knew that he didn't really understand the situation. It had taken her a while before she told him about her episodes and he'd listened and sympathised and tried to comprehend, but the connection just wasn't there. She thought it felt like trying to explain to someone who didn't believe in the supernatural that you'd seen a ghost – even if the person telling you the story is someone you love and trust, you just cannot accept it. And Rob didn't believe in any kind of supernatural phenomenon.

"I know I can," she said, "but sometimes it just doesn't seem right."

"This is the first one you've had for a while though, isn't it? Did you want to talk about it?"

"Not really."

"Well if you do," he said and put his hand on her thigh, "please say something."

She smiled, both to reassure him and shut him up. She wished she hadn't said anything now. "I will, I promise."

~

The roads stayed clear for the rest of the journey and when Rob saw the first sign for Heyton, he fiddled with the radio tuner and Beth smiled.

"I really love the fact that you do this," she said.

The tuner stopped at Classic FM and he pressed it again. "It makes me feel more like I'm away."

Tuning into the local radio station (except at home, where he stuck with Radio 2) was something Rob had been doing for as long as he'd been driving. Although most stations were the same, DJ's recruited from hospital radio and playlists that repeated themselves over the course of the day, it gave him a sense of place, the same feeling he got watching news reports from a different TV station – you saw parts of the country that you didn't normally, heard different accents and saw a world that existed all the time but which you only ever caught glimpses of.

The tuner moved up the scale and stopped at 106.6. The last few bars of "Mystify" filled the car.

"INXS there," said the DJ, overly brightly. "I'm Kit Richards and you're listening to 106.6 Heyt FM. We'll have a few adverts and then it's over to Jennifer at the newsdesk for the midday news."

Rob looked out of the window as the adverts played and caught his first glimpse of the dark blue water off the coast.

"Good afternoon, I'm Jennifer Marchant. There's still no news of youngster Toby Saddler, who went missing from Heyton on Wednesday morning. As we reported yesterday, hundreds of locals joined Toby's parents and the police to search the seafront, but no sign was found of him. The police are advising anyone with any information to come forward and his parents will be issuing an appeal later on this afternoon. This morning, our reporter Vickie Bryce spoke to Maddie, Toby's mother…"

They drove in silence, listening as Maddie tearfully explained how lovely and friendly and cheerful and helpful her son was, how he'd never done anything like this before and that if he came home, he wouldn't be in trouble.

Vickie Bryce cut in, to give a similar roundup that the newscaster had.

Rob looked at Beth, who was staring blankly at the road. It wasn't the first time that he'd ever heard this kind of thing happening, but it was the first time he'd heard it sitting next to the woman he loved, who was carrying their child.

"Not good," he said.

"No," she said, carefully and slowly, "those poor people. It's not good at all."

CHAPTER 6

BY HALF TWELVE, STEVE ELLIS felt like someone had spent the morning punching him in the head. Even the slightest of movements caused sharp pains to jab his temples and his vision kept clouding, only to clear and be punctuated by little star bursts.

At first, he thought he must be coming down with Josh's bug but his stomach had cleared up and there was no weariness or aches in his joints. It didn't make any sense.

He drove the JCB onto the loading bay of the warehouse next to The Yard, which Exeter Construction had co-opted as its site office.

Chris Valentine was standing on the dock, a clipboard in his hand and Steve groaned. It wasn't that he didn't like Valentine – he was a decent enough bloke and they'd been drivers together, once – but his promotion occasionally turned him into a jobsworth arsehole.

Steve parked and walked across the bay, heading for the office that was used as a canteen.

"Ellis," called Valentine.

Steve took a deep breath and looked up. "Chris?"

"Are you going for your break?"

"Uh huh."

"What time were you in this morning?"

He couldn't remember swiping his card and knew the printout would be on Valentine's desk on Monday morning, so he told the truth. "About half six. My kid's got a bug, I got an hour or two of sleep and I felt like shit. Sorry."

Valentine nodded. "I sympathise, really, but this isn't a charity, Steve."

"I know, I'm sorry. But he's bad, he really is." His headache had stepped up a gear as he looked at Valentine.

"Fair enough, but eat your lunch in your cab, yeah? If I let you off being late, every fucker on the beach is going to be chancing their arm, aren't they?"

Pain jabbed Steve's temples, like someone driving nails through his skull. It was all he could do to not flinch. "I suppose so."

"Good. Now bugger off and don't be late on Monday, you got it?"

"Got it," said Steve and he walked back to the JCB.

Rob turned onto the Heyton Road, a single carriageway nightmare that he remembered from previous visits – it seemed to last for miles, was impossible to overtake on and there was nothing to see except farm fields, with crops or cows or sheep and a pub about halfway along that had what Beth would no doubt call a pretty windmill behind it.

They'd made good time, having had lunch on the run – they'd pulled into some services, bought some overpriced sandwiches and shared a bottle of water.

Beth hadn't said much after the news bulletin, most of which was repeated in the next one and he hadn't tried to push her. Now, they drove along in silence, looking for quick glimpses of the sea as the land dipped here and there to show the horizon line.

He thought about Kathy. He'd only met her twice, but could see that she and Beth got on really well and they talked of each other as best friends, rather than cousins. The news of her death had shattered Beth and he'd never seen anybody cry so much. So what was he supposed to make of this episode? All of the other ones she'd told him about had been little things, most of which didn't upset her. This obviously had and he hadn't handled her announcement very well.

He tried so hard to believe, but couldn't.

The road began to slope downwards and they passed the holiday camp that he knew was on the outskirts of the town.

"Nearly there," he said and Beth looked at him. "Are you okay?"

She rubbed her belly idly. "Feeling a bit sick, to be honest. I don't know if it's breakfast, lunch, Junior or the car."

"If it's the car – and the town isn't chock-a-block with traffic – we should be at the seafront in five minutes or so."

"Good," she said and rubbed his leg.

Rob followed the signs for the sea front, driving through residential streets with expensive-looking houses, that gradually got smaller and cheaper looking until he came to the docks.

From there, he followed the town road around, past the shopping centre and turned into Sea View Road. The buildings here were tall and imposing, a college on his right, a whole row of B&B's on his left. At the end of the road, he could see the edge of the Sea Life centre. Next to it was a small blur of sand and the dark blue of the water, the sky a lighter blue above it.

Beth got the instructions sheet from the door tray and read it quickly. "Turn right," she said.

Rob turned into Marine Road and they had just driven by The Royalty Theatre when Beth suddenly pointed to the right. "There," she said.

He looked over and was pleasantly surprised. He thought it might be a little dive with aspirations above its station, but he'd been wrong. He'd seen it on previous visits and could remember wondering how much it would cost to spend a night in it.

The Clairmont Hotel was a three-storey, double-fronted building of grey brick, with a dark Mansard roof and a red-tiled tower at each corner. From the road, a long driveway curved around an ornamental garden and fountain.

"Wow," said Beth, "it's beautiful. Are you sure this is free?"

"Uh huh, with inclusive use of the restaurant and gym, if we want it."

She rubbed her hands together. "Heh, heh, bring it on. I bet you don't wish you were in Barbados now, do you?"

Rob turned into the driveway. "I wouldn't say that, love, you know?"

He parked in a space a little way from the front doors. They got out, got their luggage and walked up the wide, stone steps to check in. Once he'd shown the receptionist the instructions sheet, they were directed to the top floor, following thickly carpeted halls and staircases, the walls and ceilings lavishly ornate and gothic.

"This is lovely," said Beth, leaning close to him, as if the very splendour of the place demanded that conversations were whispered.

"Not too shabby," he said.

At the top of the stairs, he checked the keyfob. Number three was to his right, at the far end. "Looks like we have a corner room."

"Really? Do you suppose it'll be an actual tower?"

Rob smiled and shrugged, unlocked the door and pushed it open.

"It is," Beth said excitedly, "it's a circular room."

She ran in and Rob followed her. It was a large room, with four big windows overlooking the seafront, the water glittering in the sunlight. To his left was the bathroom, which Beth was looking around.

"Bath, shower, toilet," she called to him. "And it's so clean."

To his right was a king size bed, the headboard against the chimney breast with wardrobes fitted on either side into each alcove. Above the bed was a large print of a sailing ship on a calm ocean.

Beth came out of the bathroom and hugged him tightly.

"Do you like it?" he said.

"I love it. I don't think I've ever stayed in a place this plush. And look at the size of that bed."

He gave her a kiss. "I'm glad madam approves. Now did you want to check out the hotel or go for a wander in town?"

"Town first, I reckon. Let's enjoy the sunshine."

"I'm going to put my shorts on then," he said. It was too warm for jeans and T-shirts.

"Good thinking, Batman."

Rob put his rucksack on the bed and rooted through it until he found his shorts. Beth did the same, on the window side of the bed, the side that she normally slept at his place.

The sun made her a silhouette and he watched her take off her jeans and pull on her shorts. He felt like taking her in his arms there and then and making love to her. Instead, he checked the front pocket of his rucksack, to make sure that his surprise was still safe. It was, he could feel its boxy shape.

When they were dressed, Rob locked the door and they went down to the lobby.

~

Going downstairs, Beth's happiness at being away and the glamour of the hotel made her feel a lot better than she had been. Nothing was resolved, of course and she knew that it would all come flooding back, but for the moment, she was happier than she'd been in a while.

"You're enjoying this, aren't you?" he said.

"Aren't you? We thought we weren't even going to have a holiday and now we're at the seaside, on a gorgeous day, in a wonderful hotel – it's brilliant."

"I am enjoying it, but just take it easy. You don't want to knacker yourself out, do you?"

She raised her eyebrow. "Oh right, feeling a bit horny are we?"

He smiled. "I don't know if I told you this before, but sunshine and the sea air tends to have that effect on me."

"This weekend just gets better."

She hooked her arm through his and noticed a sign for the restaurant on the wall. "This must be where we get breakfast," she said and leaned through the doorway.

The dining room stretched for what seemed to be most of the length of the house, with the kitchen at the back, the doors closed now. Fifteen circular tables were dotted around the room, each with a white tablecloth and a flower in a small glass vase. They were all set for dinner and the room, with the sun streaming through the windows, looked homely and pleasant.

At first, Beth thought the room was empty but then she noticed an old woman sitting at a table next to the kitchen doors. She was gently sipping from a small china cup, her pinky finger raised.

The old woman looked up and Beth was just about to nod in acknowledgement when she felt a chill run across her shoulders. The woman looked away and Beth saw that she was dressed for winter, with fur-lined booties, a thick coat that was buttoned to the neck, a scarf and a hat pulled down firmly on her head.

The dining room wasn't cold, Beth could feel that from standing in the doorway and even though she knew old people felt the cold, it could never be this bad.

The chill slid down her back, stroking like frozen fingers. She shivered – this was wrong, all wrong. The old woman wasn't really here, she could feel that strongly and yet there she was, taking afternoon tea.

"Shall we go?" asked Rob, breaking the spell.

He was right next to her but didn't appear to have seen the old woman. Beth smiled quickly at him, to try and hide her concern.

"Yes, let's go and buy some tat," she said and they walked out into the sunshine.

~

Steve looked at his battered watch and wondered if time really was standing still.

His headache was almost blinding now, covering his scalp like a lead-lined blanket and driving up and down on the uneven sand in a noisy cab wasn't helping at all.

He wanted to be at home, with Donna and Josh, even if it meant them all laid in bed together, soothing one another's aches and pains.

Five minutes to go. Valentine, under orders from the council, was big on them getting away on time so that the beach was cleared once the kids got out of school. Compensation worries, he said.

Steve didn't mind the kids, not that he'd seen any this far along the beach, but he'd loved growing up at the seaside and remembered that part of the fun and excitement was the sense of adventure. But rules were rules and, feeling as shit as he did, he didn't mind keeping to them one little bit.

He looked at his watch again and it was almost time. He swung the JCB around and headed up towards the warehouse, to collect his wageslip and clock out.

~

Beth and Rob walked along Marine Road, nosing in the arcades and shops. Outside the Heyton Empire, he noticed the billboard for coming attractions and stopped.

"How cool is that? They're showing 'North By Northwest' tomorrow."

She smiled, knowing how much he liked Alfred Hitchcock films. "We can see it, if you want."

"Would you mind?"

"We're on holiday, let's do stuff out of the ordinary."

He draped an arm around her shoulders. "Seeing a Hitchcock film at the cinema is definitely out of the ordinary."

They walked to the junction with Commerce Street and the newsagent's had a board outside, carrying a one-sheet from the *Heyton Evening Telegraph*: 'Parents of Toby issue appeal'. They both read it, but neither made any comment. There didn't seem to be any point.

They crossed the road and Beth stopped outside a shop called Jerry's T's, flicking through a rack of tie-dyed T-shirts. Rob took the next rack and went through the T-shirts on it. He held one up and frowned. "'I Know I'm Not Mad, The Voices In My Head Told Me'? Do you suppose people really wear these things?"

"Seems like it," Beth said, tilting her head to one side.

Commerce Street was busy but he saw immediately who Beth meant. A family walked by her, talking loudly. The father was short and fat, his skin as fiery looking as his red hair and his T-shirt read 'Not As Pissed As I Should Be'. The mother, the same shape but shorter, was wearing a T-shirt with the 'Voices In My Head' design on it. Three kids were scuffing along behind them, two boys – one wearing a Leeds shirt, the other a T-shirt with a flaming skull emblazoned on it – and a young girl, who was wearing a T-shirt that said 'Slutty Angel',

Rob put the T-shirt back and Beth took his hand as they walked, weaving between the other holidaymakers.

"Hey," she said, as they passed a sweet shop, "did you fancy a nice big 99? Double flake?" "Sounds good to me."

She kissed him and went in. Rob leaned against the wall as a JCB drove past, the sun glinting off the cab windows and momentarily blinding him. Three cars were following it, the last one a taxi, the driver with a face like thunder.

~

Commerce Street was as mobbed as Steve had known it would be, but it was the quickest way back to the depot. Even though he knew that the traffic – both cars and pedestrians – would get on his nerves, he just wanted to get home.

He scanned either side of the street constantly, keeping watch for any kids that might break free of their parents' grip and dash into the road. Other than that, he didn't pay much attention to anything, even the young girls in their minimal amounts of clothes.

He turned right, where Brooks Way cut through Commerce Street and then into Sharman Drive, where the depot was.

He parked alongside the rest of the fleet, the paintwork gleaming in the sun like a shining yellow carpet and locked the cab. He posted the keys through the box, waved at the receptionist and then got into his own car. It was roasting in there, but he didn't care – at least he was one step nearer to home.

~

The Yard was empty, except for a woman cutting through to the beach, pushing a stroller. If she heard the buzzing sound as she passed the memorial, she didn't show it. Nor did she seem to notice that vibrations from the marble plate were making the chain jump, pulling on the pillars that held it up.

She was too far away to see the small puff of green smoke that broke through a crack in the marble and then she was out of sight, pushing the stroller onto the beach and kicking off her flip-flops.

Underneath the marble, in that area that was always total darkness, in that cold and dank cell of a grave, something stirred.

CHAPTER 7

STEVE PULLED UP ON his driveway, switched off the engine and rested his head on the steering wheel. His head was pounding so hard now that he felt sick and he knew headache tablets wouldn't work at all.

The pressure of the steering wheel against his forehead seemed to help slightly and he rolled his head over the hard plastic, temple to temple. With his head to the left, he saw Josh's bike, on its kickstand by the kitchen window.

How was he now? If he felt like Steve did, no wonder the kid hadn't slept well.

Donna came out of the front door, a concerned look on her face. He gave her a weak smile and got out of the car.

"You alright, love?" she asked, walking barefoot to meet him.

"I'm fine," he lied. "Just a tough day, that's all."

She gently touched his forehead. "You didn't get much sleep, did you?"

"Neither did you. How is he?"

"Well his fever's broken. I rang the doctors' first thing and got him in, but apparently there's not a lot we can do except give him Calpol. He's asleep now."

"Good," he said and reached for her hand. Her ministrations weren't doing the pain any favours at all. "What about you?"

"I feel a bit better, I've had a nap. Why don't you have a shower and a lie down?"

He walked through the door and dropped the cooler bag by the telephone table. The house was dark, the blinds in the lounge drawn against the sun and it felt cool. "I think I will, do you mind?"

"Of course not, silly. I'll wake you up later, for your tea."

He kissed her gently and stroked her fringe away from her eyes. "Thank you."

She frowned at him. "What for? I'm only protecting my man."

Steve laughed, but that hurt so he patted her backside and went up the stairs.

He opened Josh's door gently. The air smelled stale and hot – a smell he remembered from childhood, being home from school poorly with the curtains closed – as if it were taking the fever out of him, but leaving it hanging overhead like a damp blanket.

The boy was curled up under his duvet, sucking his thumb. His hair looked damp, but he was sleeping soundly and that was something.

"Get well, little man," whispered Steve and went into his and Donna's bedroom to get undressed.

The shower was both refreshing and sore, the spray feeling like it was burning his face and when he was done, he went into the bedroom, opened the window and closed the curtains. Donna had made the bed after her nap and he decided not to pull the duvet over him. He didn't feel either hot or cold and didn't want to give the room a fever-stink.

He closed his eyes and was asleep almost immediately.

~

"Did you want to go around the shopping centre?" asked Rob.

"Nah. It'll be high street shops and we can do them at home."

"Let's head back then," he said. "Go the other way?" He pointed to the road they'd come in on.

"Sounds good to me," said Beth.

As she walked, her mind began to turn things over but still her happiness at being away refused to leave. She'd had so many doubts about the weekend, knowing that her turmoil over Kathy would cast a long shadow and also that Rob wasn't really looking forward to coming here. She would have loved to go to Barbados – the guaranteed sunshine, sitting around the pool, getting a tan – but Heyton was fine. Even Rob seemed to be coming around. After all, they had a terrific hotel, it was hot and the sky was clear and blue.

The pavement branched and they could either go by some houses or through a small green. Rob guided her into the green, past well-tended rose bushes and a McMillan nurses' daffodil patch and then she heard a heavy throbbing.

She looked up at the police helicopter, the gyroscopic camera swivelling on the underside.

"I wonder if they've found him yet?" said Rob.

"I hope so," she said, remembering how she'd felt when she heard the news on the radio. It drove home, like nothing she'd felt before, what was about to happen to her. She rubbed her belly, hoping that she and Junior would never have to go through what Toby and his parents were suffering now. "I hope so."

~

Steve could feel the sun burning his skin and was about to put some more cream on when he became aware, even through his sunglasses, that the brightness penetrating his eyelids had dimmed slightly.

"Hello?"

It was a female voice, but not Donna. Slowly, he opened his eyes but could only see a black shape.

"Yeah?" he said.

"Oh. I thought you'd be pleased to see me." The voice had a hurt tone to it.

"Who are you?"

The shape moved backwards, so that he was staring straight at the sun. He screwed his eyes tightly shut but it was too late, two dancing globes of white skipped across his eyelids.

"Shit," he said and sat up, sweat running down his forehead and back.

"Well you could have at least pretended to be happy to see me."

He took off his glasses and tried to rub away the dancing globes. "Who are you?"

"Why won't you look at me? You certainly know how to make a girl feel welcome."

Steve opened his eyes and it took him a moment or two to focus on the woman, standing to his left. His eyes flickered down and he hurriedly got to his feet.

"Hi," said the woman. She was about five foot eight, with striking red hair that cascaded past her shoulders. He looked further, unable to help himself, his gaze taking in her nakedness. Her breasts were full and firm, her belly slightly rounded, her pubic hair thick. Her skin was white, without any tan marks and a line of three moles ran diagonally across her belly, starting just above her belly button.

"I'm Isabel. Why don't you lie back down?"

He glanced around, looking for Donna and Josh, but the beach was empty. The coastal defence rocks were a hundred yards to his right, but there were no JCBs or lorries to be seen.

Isabel put her cool hands against his chest. "Lie down," she said.

He did and she laid next to him. He hotched over, so that she could use the towel and she moved closer to him, her breasts pressing his side, her pubic hair tickling his thigh.

"My wife'll be here soon," he said, feeling uncomfortable, aware that his penis was stirring. "I'm not being funny, but you know…"

"No she won't," said Isabel slowly, "it's just me and thee."

"I don't know…" He stopped talking when she put her right index finger to his lips.

"Hush. We're alone." She kissed his shoulder and trailed her finger over his chin and down his neck. She put her finger in her mouth and sucked his sweat from it. He took a deep breath, fully erect. "You taste very nice, Steve."

"Thank you."

"Do you want to touch me?"

He did, more than anything. "But Donna…"

Isabel propped herself up on one elbow. "I don't like to repeat myself, Steve, so listen to me. Donna isn't here and she won't be coming along. Nor will anyone else. The only thing stopping you from doing anything is your cowardice."

"Yes," he said.

She used the same finger to circle his right nipple. "Now, do you want me?"

"Yes, Isabel, I do."

Quickly, she raised herself and laid on him, grinding her pubic bone against his. Her lips brushed his cheek and her hair fell forward, like a curtain.

"Shall I kiss you?"

"Yes," he said and she did, her tongue sliding into his mouth. He sucked on it and she drew back, then came in again and nibbled his lips.

She pushed with her hands, sliding her body over his sun-cream slicked skin, her tongue licking his chest and then circling each nipple in turn, her teeth nipping him lightly.

"Oh God," he groaned.

"He's of no use to you now."

She slid further and he reached out, cupping her breasts. They felt both firm and soft, bigger than Donna's, succulent. He wanted to taste them, to explore them with his tongue and teeth, to make her call out for God.

Isabel pushed herself down further, her breasts sliding over his trunks. He lifted his head and she smiled at him, kneeling between his legs, his erection pressing against its fabric restraint.

"Did I do this?" she asked, an innocent smile on her face.

"I think so."

She reached for the waistband of his trunks and, in one quick movement, pulled them down to his mid-thigh, his penis slapping his belly.

She touched the underside of his scrotum with her tongue, making him gasp, then licked her way to the root of his penis.

"Is this what you want?" she asked, looking at him, his quivering penis an inch for so from her chin.

"Yes, yes, it is."

"Well then, you must do something for me. I need you to promise me, before I do anything."

"Yes, I promise."

"You don't know what it is yet," she said, flicking her tongue at his scrotum.

"I don't care," he said, desperately and closed his eyes, "I'll do it."

She cupped his testicles with one hand. "I need you to give me their babies."

He opened his eyes and she flicked her tongue over the tip of his penis.

"Babies?"

"You promised me, Steve," she said and gripped his penis tightly, her hand moving up and down slowly. "I can stop right now, if you'd prefer."

"No," he said, "please don't. I'll give you their babies."

"Thank you," she said and took him in her mouth, her hands moving at the same time.

~

Steve woke up, lying on his side and rolled onto his back, his erection springing to attention.

"Holy shit," he said and rubbed his face gently.

"Steve? Are you awake?" called Donna.

He sat up quickly as she came up the stairs. His erection was harder than he could remember it being for a long time and it wasn't the kind of morning glory that Donna sometimes made affectionate fun of; this was an erection for a beautiful woman, like Isabel had revealed herself to be in his dream.

Was it a dream? It had been so realistic – he could still feel the touch of her skin, the moistness of her lips and the swell of her breasts under his fingers.

He slid around, so that his back was to the door. Donna came and sat next to him and touched the back of his neck, but her touch was wrong, her fingers weren't cool and smooth. She kissed his shoulders, but her lips weren't firm enough.

"Do you feel any better?"

He didn't know what she meant and then remembered the headache. He rubbed his temples but there was no pain. "I do," he said, "it seems to have gone."

"Brilliant," she said and kissed his shoulder again. "Josh is up and about now too, but he's not recovered like you have. Why don't you get dressed and come down for some tea?"

He nodded, hoping she'd go away. He didn't want her to see his erection, because she would guess it was for someone else and he didn't want her to touch him any more – he didn't like how her skin felt against his.

"Come down when you're ready, yes?"

"Yes," he said and endured another kiss – on the top of his head this time – before she went.

He looked at the curtains and rubbed his face hard.

"Holy shit," he said.

~

Beth looked at the hotel and Rob came up behind her, picked her up and swung her around.

"Hey, gorgeous, have I told you today how lovely you are?"

She laughed and kissed him. "Not yet."

He put her down and bent forward, his face against her belly. "And so are you, my little one."

Her heart soared and she felt warm inside. "That was nice."

"Nice bloke," he said, smiling up at her.

"Yeah, yeah. Come on, let's go and see what's for dinner."

He rubbed her belly gently, took her outstretched hand and followed her into the lobby. The reception desk was unmanned, so they walked down the corridor to the dining room.

The old woman was at the same table, still dressed for winter and sipping her tea. Beth saw her straight away and felt her arms speckle with gooseflesh, the hairs standing on end. Everything around her seemed to fade, except for the old woman.

She felt Rob free his hand.

"I'll go and see if there's a menu at reception," he said, his voice sounding like a bad connection.

"Uh huh," she muttered.

The old woman looked up but didn't acknowledge her.

"You can see her, can't you?" said someone beside her.

Beth jumped and turned quickly.

"Sorry, my dear, I didn't mean to startle you."

"No, no, that's fine."

The old woman in front of Beth smiled. She was small, less than five foot, with steel grey hair that had been expensively set quite recently. Stick thin, she was wearing a shiny blue summer dress, with huge rose petals decorating it. Her face was long and narrow, the skin lined, her lips a bright red.

"What's your name, young lady?"

"Beth."

"Pleased to meet you, Beth, I'm Rosie. I didn't mean to scare you, but you can see her, can't you?"

"What do you mean?"

"Old Goody June," said Rosie. She raised her liver spotted right hand and, with an arthritis crooked finger, pointed into the dining room. "Her."

Beth looked, but the old woman had gone.

"Ah," said Rosie, "she does that a lot. What did you see?"

"An old woman drinking tea, dressed like it was the middle of winter."

Rosie nodded. "That's her," she said and looked at Beth. "Did she scare you?"

"No, not really. So who is she?"

"I think," Rose said gravely, "that she's just another soul that hasn't passed over yet."

"A ghost, you mean?"

Rosie glanced around, as if to make sure no-one was near. Beth looked towards reception, where the girl behind the counter was showing Rob something on a piece of paper.

"Not a ghost in a white sheet saying boo, no. A lost soul, I think. I've seen and felt enough in my time to believe that souls don't always leave this mortal coil, like they're supposed to. People see strange things all the time, but dismiss them as tricks of the light. I think that what they see are the souls of people who have passed on but left their imprint, where it remains until whatever should happen, does happen. Goody June is replaying a memory from when she was alive and in this hotel taking afternoon tea. She's not haunting anyone – heck, most people can't even see her – it's just that this is what she remembers and she doesn't know to do anything else."

Beth leaned against the doorframe, after glancing over to make sure that Goody June hadn't reappeared.

"Something's troubling you, isn't it, my dear?" Rosie was staring at her with watery eyes. "A friend of yours? No, someone closer, a cousin perhaps?"

Beth felt her mouth open, but couldn't stop it and instinctively put her hands on her belly.

"Don't fret, I'm not trying to scare you."

"You didn't, I was just…" She was just what? "It's been a weird few weeks and we saw a couple of things on the way here that upset me and then there's that poor little boy."

"Aye, the Saddler boy. Sad business that. I've lived here most of my life and seen a lot of young ones disappear over the years, but it doesn't get any easier to deal with. It affects everybody, it's like a big cloud of nastiness that hangs over the town and will do until the boy is found, one way or the other."

"A cloud?"

"Can't you feel it?" Rosie asked and Beth shook her head. "It's like everyone's worries join together, to make a dark storm cloud. It's always the same. Most worries drift away, but this kind of thing – a child going missing – affects us all, deep in our souls and the horrible feelings just gather together."

"And you can feel this now?"

Rosie leaned towards Beth, her voice dropping to a whisper. "I feel something, Beth, like bad energy. I don't know what it is yet, but I don't think it's very nice."

"What do you mean, not nice?"

"I have to go," said Rosie, "take my medication and have a lie down. You be careful now, you hear?"

"I will," said Beth, quietly. "And thank you."

Rosie waved at her and hobbled away towards the staircase.

"Roast dinner tonight," said Rob. Beth looked at him, surprised to see him. "Hey, you okay?" he asked.

"Um? Yes, I was just talking to this old woman." Beth pointed towards the stairs, but couldn't see any sign of Rosie. "Oh, she must have gone up already."

"Okay," said Rob, easily. "Well dinner's at six, so do you want to get freshened up first?"

"Yes," said Beth, glancing back into the dining room, which was still empty. "That'd be good."

"Are you sure you're okay?" Rob sounded concerned.

"I'm fine," said Beth firmly, not quite sure what had just happened to her.

CHAPTER 8

DONNA COOKED BANGERS AND mash, which they ate watching the TV. When they'd finished, Josh went for another lie down and Steve carried the plates into the kitchen.

"Are you feeling better now?" asked Donna, filling the sink with hot water.

He was, but had the horrible feeling that his dream was responsible for it. Not that he could remember a lot of it now. "Yes, thanks."

"Good. Did you fancy renting a DVD tonight?"

"I can't, I'm going out." He paused – he hadn't realised he was going to say that until he did. "Sorry."

"You didn't say. Where're you going?"

He shrugged. "The Embassy Rooms, with some of the lads from work. The Flayed are playing."

Donna screwed up her face. "Really? Shit, I'd love to see them again. Why didn't you say earlier, we could have arranged a sitter."

"Sorry, love. Anyway, I'm going to get changed and get going."

"But it's not even half seven."

"Time waits for no man," he said and gave her a kiss.

He went upstairs, unsure of exactly what he was doing. Was his recovery short-lived, the fever burrowing into his brain? Perhaps he shouldn't be going out tonight after all.

He thought about it as he splashed on some aftershave and got dressed.

～

The Yard, once again, was empty.

Nothing moved, no birds flew overhead and no litter blew across the grass.

The vibrations began around the memorial, the marble moving slightly and nudging the in-memorium stones, which rattled the pillars. The chain, with Steve's botched-up repair job, danced lightly and it would have looked like the effect of a breeze had anyone seen it.

The crack in the marble widened slightly as green smoke began to filter through. It moved upwards, winding itself around the granite spike and slowly coalesced into the shape of a woman.

Isabel Mundy's form didn't see The Yard or Marine Road, only Steve Ellis picking a shirt out of his wardrobe.

She smiled.

Soon, she knew, the people of Heyton would feel her wrath.

~

By eight o'clock, Steve was ready. He was wearing his Valentino shirt, a pair of chinos and the Pod shoes Donna had bought him from one of the discount warehouses by the docks. He looked at himself in the mirror, slotting the last few buttons into their holes.

Donna came in and stood behind him, helping him out. "You're looking good. And smelling good. Hoping for a little action?"

'*Your wife won't be along in a while, it's just me and you here.*'

Donna didn't seem to have heard the voice. "Nah, I'm strictly a one-woman man, you know that."

She laughed and patted his bum. "One woman at a time, you mean?"

"The logistics are too complicated with three people. Someone's always going to get left out."

Donna stood on tiptoes and kissed his cheek. "Well you have a good time. And be careful."

"I will. I mean, what could happen to me?"

~

Beth stood on the wall that separated Marine Road from the pathway above the beach and looked at the golden colours of the sunset. It looked magical and she hoped that Rob's camera caught what they could see.

The air filled with a familiar whup-whup sound and she looked up, expecting to see the police helicopter, but it was an Air-Sea-Rescue unit flying along the line of the water's edge. It disappeared out of sight behind the pier.

Rob stood up and brushed sand from his knee. "Do you suppose they're looking for him?"

"I don't know," she said and got off the wall.

Rob climbed over from the pathway and touched her arm. "They'll probably find him. When I was talking to the receptionist earlier, she said a dozen or more kids go missing here every year and nine times out of ten they turn up safe and sound."

"It'd be horrible to be the tenth parent, wouldn't it?"

"Hey," he said and put his arm around her, "stop thinking like that. These people know what they're doing. He'll turn up, he's probably having the time of his life somewhere."

"I seriously doubt that, Rob."

He nodded. "Me too. But there's nothing we can do."

He was right, but the thought of suffering an ordeal like this pricked at her, as did Rosie's proclamation of a dark cloud. She rubbed her belly and knew she was probably working herself up for nothing. She'd seen a picture of Toby in some of the shops and was keeping an eye out for him – that was all she could do. "So, change of subject. How many shots have you got left?"

He checked the window. "Three. Why, did you want to do some tasteful sunset nudes?"

"What, before I get all big and fat?"

"Who's talking about big and fat? You're going to be gorgeous when you're eight or nine months gone."

"Yeah, yeah, all big and fat."

"Hey, come on. Stand there and let me take a picture of you against the sunset."

"It'll never come out."

"But I can lighten it up in the computer."

"Alright," she said and sat on the wall.

He lined the shot up and took the picture, the flash blinding her. "Shit," he said, "I forgot to switch off the flash."

She stood up and dusted off her behind. "Well don't waste anymore, we'll take some later."

"Okay," he said and took her hand and led her past the municipal pool to the road.

~

Steve walked to the end of his street with a confident gait but something was nagging at the back of his mind.

What was he doing? Why had he lied to Donna? He hadn't arranged to see the lads from work and didn't even know if the Flayed were actually playing at the Embassy Rooms.

He stood on the corner and decided to ignore his misgivings and head towards Marine Road anyway.

As he walked, nodding at neighbours who were coming back from the beach in the gathering dusk, his headache suddenly came back so intensely that he had to stop and lean against a wall. He pressed his fingers to his temples, squinting his eyes against the pain, willing it to stop.

He is pushed into the hole, the stone cold against his naked back and buttocks. He can see a slab of sky and then several angry men's faces appear in front of it and he recognises one of them, feels something for him, but the man spits on him and that feeling fades, like mist on a sunny morning.

He screams for them to leave him alone and it's not his voice still. He uses phrases like "please, stop," or "have mercy on me" but they have no effect.

"She done?" asks someone and he watches, terrified, as another stone is pushed over the gap. He can hear the rasp of it as his view of the sky gets thinner until it's gone completely and he's in darkness and all he can hear is his own gasping breath.

Steve tilted his head, hearing the tendons in his neck creak, his headache clearing. He knew now why he was going into town.

~

Beth swung the steering wheel right around and all she could hear for a couple of moments was the horrible screaming of the tyres as they struggled to stay on the tarmac.

"Shit," she said and swung the wheel back the other way when the car began to slide.

She caught the skid and got the car straight, putting her foot down to try and catch the others.

Glancing up at Rob, she raised her eyebrows. The kid next to her said, "Good turn" and then he hunched over his own wheel and tried to catch her up.

They were in the Slot-Time arcade and Rob leaned against Beth's monitor as she raced around a Sega test track with three others – the kid, a teenager and a man in his early twenties, whose bored looking girlfriend leaned against his seat and alternately looked at his monitor and her nails.

Rob wasn't a big fan of arcades, but he enjoyed "House Of The Dead" and had come in to play that. Beth loved racing games, so she'd stood and watched him play out his pound and now he was watching her do the same.

She turned into the final stretch, the clock counting down faster now than it had before and he smiled at the look of concentration on her face. The kid next to her was pulling on his steering wheel, so that he could push down harder on the accelerator pedal but he wasn't going to get past her.

The clock was at five when she sped over the finishing line. Her car did a neat circle and the virtual camera zoomed in on it as a garland appeared around it.

She laughed and Rob helped her out of the moulded plastic seat.

"Hammond strikes again," she said, "the reporters are waiting in packs in the paddock but still she refuses to reveal her secret as to why she keeps on winning."

"Isn't it skill?" said Rob.

"Rob Warren, the BBC's expert sports-reporter bangs the nail on the head. Yes, of course it's skill, but as I'm the first successful woman rally driver, I have to be modest."

Rob laughed. "You finished?"

"Yes," she said, grinning widely, "shall we go?"

Darkness was settling over Heyton, with only a few streaks of red left in the sky. All of the arcades on Marine Road were lit up brightly and bingo callers, their loudspeakers near the doors, extolled the benefits of playing their game rather than anyone else's.

Rob followed Beth out of the door and watched as the lights played across her body. "Let me get a picture of you now, you look lovely with all of these lights on you."

She shrugged. "If that's what you want."

He stood at the kerb and took his camera from its pouch. He looked up and Beth was striking a pose, which made him laugh. He took the picture and the film finished, the auto-rewind humming and making the camera vibrate in his hand.

"Damn, I thought I had another shot," he said.

"I think I saw a chemist's on the corner earlier. Why don't we put the film in and then head back for the hotel."

"It's only about nine, don't you want to go anywhere else?"

She cuddled into him as they walked. "No. I remember someone telling me earlier that the sea air and sunshine made him horny and I wanted to test it out."

"Let's find that chemist's."

The newsagent's on the corner of Commerce Street was closed, the board inside now. The chemist's was next door and its door guard was halfway down, though the opening times on the window indicated the shop was open for another half an hour.

Rob crouched down and pushed the door. "Are you open?" he asked the man behind the counter.

The man, barely out of teens, looked up. "Uh huh, unless you want a prescription filling."

"No, just a film to be developed."

"I can't do it tonight, but we open at eight tomorrow if you want to do the hour service?"

"That'll be fine," said Rob and handed over the cartridge.

The man filled in the forms and handed over a ticket, which Beth took. "I'll be up first," she said, "trust me."

The man and Rob looked at one another and smiled.

"Nine o'clock tomorrow," said the man.

"I'll be here," said Beth.

CHAPTER 9

WHEN STEVE REACHED THE Embassy Rooms, he couldn't see clearly. Some dickhead had taken a picture of his girlfriend outside the Slot-Time arcade and he'd been caught in it, the flash blinding him.

Fucking tourists, he thought, why take a picture there? It's not as if it'd look wonderful on the mantelpiece, is it?

"Steve-o," said the doorman, a hulk in a black bomber jacket, earpiece and number one haircut.

"Hey, Elvis, how's it going?"

The doorman looked left and right. "Not bad. Some tasty bits on the strip tonight, are you coming in to try your luck?"

Steve sighed. "No, Elvis, I'm married aren't I? You came to the wedding."

Elvis shrugged. "Different strokes, you know? I could turn a blind eye."

"There's no need, honestly."

"Fair enough, pal," said Elvis and he held the door open.

Steve went into the lobby, paid his money and pushed through the double doors into the main area.

The Embassy Rooms had been in Heyton for as long as Steve could remember, through many incarnations – some successful, most not. At the moment, it was trying to be an 80s style disco – all neon tubing and portraits of glamorous women with big hair and bigger chests. The dance floor was a huge, circular thing with the DJ booth and a stage at the far end and tables around the side. The bar was at the back, to the left of the main door.

He looked around, taking in as much as he could as strobe lights illuminated every nook and cranny. He went to the bar and ordered a Bud, trying to figure out his next move to make sure that he pleased Isabel. That was the most important thing now – he wanted to please her, so that he could feel her against him again. But how would he know a woman was pregnant? Donna hadn't shown until she was almost six months gone and he didn't want to hurt anyone unnecessarily.

But that doesn't matter.

"What?" The voice was close to his ear. Or was it closer than that? Actually inside his head.

I want their babies. If people are hurt along the way, then so be it.

"I can't hurt someone for no reason."

You can if you want to please me.

He thought about it. "I want to please you, Isabel."

Then do as I ask.

At that moment, a group of women came through the door, the one in the lead festooned with blown up condoms, L plates and a wedding veil clipped to her hair. He watched as the rest of the hen party came through and saw her.

He thought back to a conversation at the dinner table a few weeks back. Donna had seen her in town, found out she was in the family way and over the moon about it. They'd been trying for ages.

Mandy Valentine, the wife of Chris.

"Isabel, I have one."

Don't let me down and I will give you as much pleasure as you can stand.

"I won't let you down," he said and watched the hen party move to a table and sit down.

~

Rob put his hands behind his head, trying to get comfortable enough to watch the TV without cricking his neck. The bed was wide, but it was harder than his and lying still comfortably wasn't easy.

Finally, having moved enough that the sheets were rucked up beneath him, he gave up.

Beth was in the bathroom and the TV volume was down low. From outside, he could hear people on Marine Road. The funfair had stopped about half an hour ago and everyone seemed to have left, especially those who spent all their time screaming.

He wondered whether, if you lived here all the time, you got immune to screams, as he was to house and car alarms. It wasn't the most pleasant thought he'd had all day.

The bathroom door opened and the light clicked off, leaving only the bedside lamps lit. Beth stood naked in the doorway and Rob sat up.

"Hey, gorgeous."

"I don't think much to this mirror," she said, "seeing yourself pee isn't the nicest sight in the world."

"Didn't happen to me."

Beth got onto the bed, lying beside him and stroking patterns on his chest. "So then, Mr Warren, how're we doing this evening?"

"Not bad at all, Ms Hammond," he said and stroked the small of her back, his fingers brushing the cleft of her buttocks.

"Have you enjoyed the day?" she asked, walking her fingers down his stomach.

"Uh huh. Have you?"

"Yes." Her fingers slid over his penis. "And does the sea air and sun still make you horny?"

He breathed in deeply. "Oh yes."

"How much?"

"Let me show you," he said and twisted around, pushing her onto her back.

~

Steve checked his watch. It was half past midnight and most of the clientele were drunk and staggering around.

The hen party was well on its way to getting smashed, except for Mandy Valentine. Sometime earlier, she had taken to ordering the drinks – possibly because no-one else could remember anything once they'd taken three steps from the table – and he'd watched her every move.

Now she was coming back for another round. He moved sideways, to open a slot at the bar and she stood next to him.

"Hi," he said.

She was Donna's height, her blonde hair short and feathered towards her face. If Donna was right – and why wouldn't she be? – then Mandy wasn't showing at all. Her shimmery black dress clung to her and there was no real bulge at her belly.

"Hi." She looked at him. "Do I know you?"

"Perhaps. I work on the beach with Chris."

"Ah," she said and smiled. She looked good when she smiled. "And you are?"

"Todd," he said. "I run one of the trucks."

"Great," she said, trying to cut short the conversation. She waved to get the barmaid's attention.

"Are you here with Chris?"

"No, it's Carla Davenport's hen night, so I'm here with that crowd. I'm buying the drinks because they're all as pissed as farts."

"Fair enough. Did you want a hand taking the drinks back?"

"Would you mind? Some of the people in here are as smashed as my crowd, I probably won't get everything back in one piece."

"It'd be my pleasure," he said and waited for the barmaid to finish the order, which took up two trays. "You carry that one," he indicated the lighter tray, "and I'll follow you."

They had almost reached the table without incident when someone pushed their chair back and caught Mandy's hip, knocking her sideways. The tray tilted and half a dozen glasses dropped onto the table, spraying the people sitting around it.

"Fuck," Steve heard someone say.

"My dress," said someone else.

"Ah shit," said the man who'd bumped Mandy, "why don't you watch where you're fucking going, you stupid bint?"

"You knocked me, it's your fault."

A woman, wearing a pastel coloured short dress that was now stained dark with drink, stood up and rubbed at her lap. "You stupid bitch, look what you've done to me."

"Hey," said Steve, "it's not her fault."

The man turned to him. "Are you planning to make something of it?"

"No, I'm trying to get things clear. We don't want any trouble."

"But my bird's drenched and it's your bint's fault."

Steve took a deep breath. "It's not and you know it. Come on, mate, sit down."

"Yeah, right," said the man and drew his arm back. It was grabbed by another hand and Steve recognised the sovereign rings on each finger. Elvis to the rescue.

Except it didn't happen that way. With his hand drawn back, the man lost his balance and fell onto Elvis, who fell back himself against someone else.

The man got up and tried to clobber Elvis, who sidestepped and the punch caught a woman above her ear. Instantly, the woman's boyfriend was on his feet, fists ready. Elvis spoke rapidly into his mouthpiece and Steve reached forward and touched Mandy's shoulder, making her jump and turn slightly.

"I think it might be wise to get out of here."

She was looking, open mouthed, at the fight, which was taking on a life of its own. "What about my friends?"

The hen party were standing on their chairs to get a better view, some of them cheering the fighters on. "I think they'll be safe."

Another drinker, not involved at all yet, threw a punch at Elvis, who ducked.

Steve pulled Mandy back. "Come on, this is going to kick off big time." He put his hand in the small of her back and propelled her towards the main doors. Just before they reached them, half a dozen bouncers came through, murder in their eyes.

Then Steve and Mandy were through, standing on the pavement in the warm night air.

"That was lucky," he said.

She started laughing. "That all came out of nothing, didn't it?"

"It usually does. Come on, I'll walk you home."

"No, it's okay, I'll get a taxi."

"Don't be so silly, I can walk you."

She looked at him nervously. "Todd, seriously, I can get a taxi."

"You don't have to worry about anything, I won't attack you. It's a nice evening, we can get some air and then Chris won't be worried that you get home too early."

Mandy considered this. "You're right. He might want to know what happened if I get back too early."

"And he probably wouldn't be all that happy if you nearly got beaten up in a fight."

75

"No, you're right. But where do you live?"

"Hampton Close," Steve lied, "what about you?"

"Garrison Avenue. So we're not too far from each other."

"Decision made then. We can cut through Ragsdale and then we don't have to risk any more trouble on the strip or in town."

"Sounds good to me," she said and they started to walk.

As they passed the Clairmont, she stopped and undid her shoes. "These are killing me," she said, sitting on a wall and rubbing the soles of her feet.

Steve waited for her to stand up, holding her shoes in front of her. He'd decided where he was going to do the deed. The Fair was deserted now, the rides all locked up, the lights off. That had to be the best spot, since it was far enough away from the strip that, with the music rumbling out of the pubs and clubs, people probably wouldn't hear the struggles.

They began to walk, the Log Flume across the road from them.

"You alright now?"

"Yeah. I don't know why I wear these shoes, they really kill my feet."

"My wife's got these shoes that she loves, but she can only wear them for about an hour."

"Vanity," said Mandy. "We want to look good and who cares if it's painful."

"Women and pain is a strange thing, isn't it? They seem to be able to stand a lot more than men."

She looked at him, suddenly nervous again. "Like what?"

"Well, I don't know, like wearing bad shoes and having kids and the like."

"I don't have any kids yet."

"But one's on the way, isn't it?"

She looked back towards the pubs and clubs on the strip, as if just realising how far away she was from people who were awake. "How did you know that?"

He realised he'd made a slip. "Chris told me."

"No he didn't, you're a liar, Todd." Something seemed to click within her. "If you are Todd."

"Ah, fuck this," he said and punched her in the face.

She fell, sprawling against the car park wall. "You fucking punched me," she screamed, touching her left cheek gently. "You fucking arsehole, what do you…"

Steve knelt down and leaned close to her. "Keep your voice down, or things'll get a lot worse."

"Worse?"

"Trust me," he said and lifted her to her feet. He put her over his shoulder and crossed the road towards the Fair.

~

Mandy's head was pounding, her cheekbone singing out in agony. She didn't think it was broken, but it hurt like hell. Also, she couldn't breathe properly, his shoulder was digging into her belly and ribs. All she could think about, aside from the pain, was what he might do to her or the baby. She had to fight him, give as good as she got and save herself.

But his shoulder dug into her wickedly. With every step, her capacity to draw breath got less. Suddenly, she felt sick and the edge of her vision fluttered. No, not now, she couldn't let herself pass out. She bit the inside of her uninjured cheek hard enough to draw blood.

She looked around as best she could. He followed the bund wall around the Log Flume and then stopped. She heard metal rattling against metal and realised they must be at the gates to the Fair.

"Where are you taking me?" she managed to gasp.

"Don't worry, you've got nothing to worry about at all."

"Please Todd," she gasped, "please don't hurt me."

"I won't," he said and, without warning, let go of her. She landed on her shoulder and side and rolled onto her back, looking up at the sky. She rested her head against the cool concrete, her cheekbone throbbing with pain.

The rattling sounded again and she looked up. Todd, if that's who he was, was pulling at the padlock that held the big iron gates closed. The movement rattled a sign, hung between the two. It showed a smiling clown face, with huge cheeks and eyes and, curved over his head, was the legend 'Heyton Funfair: The Time Of Your Life!!'.

CONJURE

Todd pressed something against the padlock and pulled. She heard a click and he pulled the right hand gate open slightly.

"Come on," he said and pulled her to her feet.

He shoved her through the gate and she fell to her knees, the concrete scraping them. She wanted to cry out, but fear had robbed her of a voice. Different scenes played in her head, all of them sickening. Out here, he could do whatever he wanted, violate her how he chose and nobody would hear, even if she screamed at the top of her lungs.

She had to get away.

Mandy rolled into a sitting position and watched Todd, his back to her, put the gate back and loop the chain through its clasps. The lights from the street faced him and inside the fair there weren't any lights at all, except for a single band of Christmas lights strung across the top of the rollercoaster.

This was her chance.

She got to her feet and rubbed her left temple gingerly. Her head and cheek were throbbing and she felt sick, but she had to shut that away somehow, had to get out of here.

Once she'd steadied herself, she ran quickly towards one of the stalls that lined the street side of the Fair, her bare feet making the lightest slapping noises on the concrete. The stalls were arranged with an accessway between each one, so that the vendor could get into them. She looked at the first stall, realised he would check there straight away and backed away from it, past the next and the next. Todd was still fiddling with whatever he was doing, content that she wouldn't be able to get away.

Mandy didn't believe she could get away but that didn't mean that she had to offer herself to him. If she could hide somewhere until morning, when the Fair opened, at least she'd have tried her best.

He began to whistle tunelessly and that, more than anything, brought her to her senses. Whatever he'd said about not hurting her, he was enjoying himself.

She backed into the fourth stall, the edge of a ledge digging into her side and bit back a gasp. This was far enough. Guiding herself with her hands, she backed to the edge of the stall and up the accessway, squatting down to make herself as small as possible. It was pitch black here, the light from the street drowned out by the two stalls being so close to one another.

The floor felt soft and mushy and smelled like rancid onions. The stall holders lunch, or a burger stand?

"Fuck," shouted Todd, "you fucking bitch." She heard his footsteps. "Where are you?"

She wouldn't give herself away for all the tea in China but put her hand over her mouth all the same, wincing as her fingertips brushed her cheek. Her breathing and heartbeat suddenly sounded too loud and that scared her. Would he hear either?

She closed her eyes, wishing she'd never agreed to come out on the hen night, that she was at home now in bed with Chris.

"Mandy!" He sounded angry and frustrated and she knew that any chance of mercy had now evaporated.

"You stupid bitch, I've locked the gates. What are you going to do, climb over them?"

Her breathing was becoming more and more rapid and she tried to calm herself down. His voice was getting closer but there was no way that he could tell where she was. He'd been turned around long enough that she could have gone anywhere in the Fair, could even now be climbing up onto the rollercoaster.

A siren began to wail in the distance and her heart skipped a beat. She knew they weren't coming for her – unless someone had seen him lay her out on the street – but she hoped against hope they were.

The siren got louder, splashes of red and blue light painting the fence. She saw her own foot and a sudden fear gripped her. If the car stopped outside, its lights might show her position.

Keeping as quiet as possible, she pressed closer to the edge of the stall and peered through the slats in the fence as the police car sped past, in a blur of noise and lights.

It wasn't coming for her, it must be heading for the Embassy Rooms.
Shit.

Todd began to laugh heartily. "Did you think help was on its way then? Afraid not. It's just you and me, love, so why not come out and we can get on?"

The temptation to scream at him was almost overwhelming and she pressed her hand tighter to her mouth, ignoring the pains that shot through her cheek.

His footsteps sounded loud as he walked along the stalls, rapping his knuckles on the ledges. "You really don't want to piss me off, Mandy and I'm already not a happy camper."

He was going to find her. He had hours before the place opened, he could make his way slowly around the Fair, climbing onto the rides if need be – he could cover the place before dawn.

With her free hand, she felt around her feet, but there was only mushy stuff and nothing like a rock or brick or even a bit of wood to throw at the bastard. Unless the mushy stuff was actually onions. She could smack him in the eyes with it, which might buy her some time. But to what end? If she didn't knock him down, he'd just come at her more angry and then she'd never get away.

He slapped the side of a stall and the sound was loud and shocking. She was glad her hand was clasped tight to her mouth, because she heard the "oh" sound she'd made involuntarily through it.

"Last chance to come out, Mandy and have the nice Todd. Come on."

Her eyes scanned the floor as she realised she was finally getting some night vision. The mush was food – half a bun, a bit of burger and plenty of salad and onions. She gathered up a handful.

He slapped the side of her stall and she felt the vibration through the wood, where her head was rested against it.

"Alright, you bitch, that does it. I wasn't going to hurt you before, but now I am. I'm going to take your clothes off, one piece at a time and bite your fucking nipples off. Do you hear me?" His voice was getting louder and the menace in it was clear.

His knuckles rapped the ledge, coming closer all the time. She was as far back as she could get but, if her night vision was kicking in, then so was his. It might take him a few moments to see her, crouched back here in a dead end like a frightened rabbit, but he would see her.

Then what would she do?

The rapping of his knuckles stopped and she saw him, vague against the dark sky, at the mouth of the accessway.

"Mandy?" he said quietly.

She kept quiet, willing him to move on. But he didn't and she watched his shape in the gloom. He crouched down, leaned forward and shielded his eyes with his hand.

"Is that really you?"

Her breath caught and her whole head began to throb. Perhaps it was a trick, perhaps he was just trying to catch her out.

"Mandy?"

No, ignore him, stay still. He can't see you, he doesn't know you're here, he's just hoping for the best.

Todd stepped into the accessway. "There you are," he said, his voice calm and gentle. "Why didn't you come out when I called you?"

As he got closer, she tried to gauge if she could get around him.

"It's rude not to speak when spoken to," he said. "If you were going to be any kind of mother, you'd know that."

She let go of her mouth and grabbed another handful of mush. One more step and she'd let him have it and then try, as best as she could, to get away.

"Speak to me," he yelled, making her jump.

She screamed and lurched forward but wasn't prepared for the wave of dizziness that washed over her. She felt herself slump sideways and her head rapped off the wood.

He laughed and she stood up straight and threw the mush at his face as hard as she could. He gave a disgusted, pained cry and reached for her, his hand hooking into the left strap of her dress. She pushed off the wall and lunged to her right, banging into the next stall. He kept coming forward, his fingers dragging on her skin and she pushed down on his shoulders.

He went down on his knees with a grunt, tearing the strap off her dress and she slid over his back. He went flat and she fell off him, landing awkwardly and twisting her ankle.

She cried out – it hurt like hell but she couldn't stay here, her chances of getting away were virtually nil anyway, but would be better if she at least got up. Gritting her teeth and using the stall for support, she stood up but couldn't put any weight on her foot.

She hadn't even managed to hobble two steps before he caught her and pushed her forward. She sprawled on the ground, her chin grazing the concrete and began to cry.

"Nice try, Mandy," said Todd and dug his hands into her armpits, pulling her to her feet in one smooth motion.

~

"I have her," Steve called, looking up into the sky.

Good. Bring her to me. There is a gap in the fence, I shall be waiting for you.

"I can't stand up," Mandy said, her voice hitching with sobs. "My ankle really hurts."

He put her left arm over his shoulder and pulled her alongside him, making her cry out in pain. "Shouldn't have tried to run off, should you?"

"Please let me go, Todd, I promise I won't tell anyone about this."

He ignored her and led her deeper into the fair, past the Ghost Train and Hi-Energy, the Funhouse and a shooting gallery. The rollercoaster loomed to his left and he went left at the Helter Skelter, past more side-stalls, a small go-carting tracks and the dodgems.

He thought about this place and remembered being here with a child, but couldn't make out who it was or when. It had been someone important, but his mind couldn't quite reach the link – about that or much else. His name was Steve Ellis, he was sure of that, but right now, all he knew was that he had to take this woman to The Yard to give her to Isabel. Beyond that, everything was a blank and that scared and excited him at the same time.

The Fair ended behind the dodgems, separated from The Yard by a section of chain-link fence. He pushed Mandy forward and she bounced off the fence and slid down in a heap.

The gap was to her right, the weight of her body pushing the slit open. He smiled – she'd helped him out, finally.

He knelt beside her and she cringed, trying to sidle sideways out of his reach.

"Through here," he said and she let out an anguished sob. "Come on, get through here."

"Please don't make me do anything else."

"If I have to push you through," he said, through gritted teeth, "then it's going to hurt you a lot more than if you do it yourself."

Mandy tried to get herself under control, but the sobs continued. "Where?" she asked, finally.

He pushed her hand against the gap. "There."

She got onto all fours and crawled through and as soon as her feet were clear, he followed.

The Yard was deserted, the yellow glow of the street light at the entrance casting long shadows across the grass and memorial. The only movement was in the bushes along the access road, which rustled slightly in a soft breeze and the only sound was the gentle rush of waves.

Steve looked around and it was like he was seeing the place for the first time, coming upon this oasis of beauty with fresh eyes uncluttered by the glitz and shiny phoniness of the strip.

He looked at the memorial and was disgusted to see that someone had broken one of the small pillars, the chain lying useless on the stones.

"We're here," he said and the memorial briefly seemed to glow a pale green.

Bring her to me.

He knelt down next to Mandy, who was still on all fours, staring at the memorial, her mouth open. It seemed as if he wasn't the only person who'd seen the glow.

"Come on, it's time for you to meet Isabel."

"No," she said, "no, no," her voice getting louder.

He reached for her but she swung her arm at his shins and must have caught him with her rings because he felt a sudden, stabbing pain there and whatever pretence of keeping his temper he'd had before, he lost now.

He roared at her, a wordless howl, grabbed a handful of her hair and strode over to the memorial, Mandy trying to keep up with him. He let go of her when he reached the chain and she fell forward.

Thank you, my familiar, you have done well.

He stepped back and Mandy rolled over. She looked at him, her cheeks streaked with tears, her chin grazed and bloody, a terrified expression on her face. "Where are you going? Who are you talking to?"

Steve backed into the fence. "You'll see," he said.

The ground began to vibrate, taking him by surprise and Mandy cried out in fear. She tried to scuttle backwards as smoke filtered through the marble.

"What is that?" she screamed, but he just shrugged. He didn't want to help her, but he also didn't know. The Steve here now had no recollection of this morning's incident with the JCB and the Steve that had wasn't in control any more.

The smoke gathered into a shape that was hard to determine at first. Mandy was still trying to scuttle backwards, but didn't seem to be getting anywhere.

Hold her for me.

He pushed himself off the fence and walked over to Mandy, grabbed her ankles and dragged her back to the memorial. She tried to kick out, but his grip was firm. Her dress rode up, her panties pulled tight in the gusset, but it didn't do anything for him. No woman could touch him in the same way that he knew Isabel could.

He glanced over his shoulder and his mouth opened. Isabel was standing in front of the memorial, naked, her hair draped over her shoulders and partially covering her breasts.

"It's good to see you," he said.

She smiled. *Soon we can be together.*

He let go of Mandy's legs and she grunted with surprise.

Isabel gestured for him to move away, so he bowed and went back to the fence.

As soon as Mandy saw Isabel, she screamed and kept on, as Isabel went to her on all fours. Mandy tried to move herself but Isabel grabbed her ankles and kept her still.

"Leave me alone," yelled Mandy, reaching for Steve, her fingers grasping uselessly. "Oh my God, Todd, help me."

Isabel stroked Mandy's legs and thighs and flattened her hands, rubbing them across Mandy's belly.

Your town has done me wrong, woman.

Steve heard every word, but Mandy screamed all the way through them.

It is your price to pay.

Isabel pressed her hands into Mandy's belly then drew back, until they were about a foot away. Wisps of green smoke, like streamers, hung from her fingertips.

Mandy screamed in pain and reached for Steve again, her eyes imploring him.

Isabel got to her knees as the streamers grew thicker and Steve heard the anguished squall of a baby from somewhere. The sound made him think of someone close to him but, again, he couldn't make the connection.

Mandy screamed once more and then her eyes rolled up to show the whites.

The squalls got louder and then Steve saw the baby, coming through Mandy's belly – the head, then the shoulders and arms. Isabel pulled back, her hands above her head, dragging the infant out.

Mandy convulsed, her head lolling in the grass and Steve gripped the chain-link, terrified, not able to fully take in what he was seeing.

Isabel stood up as the baby's kicking legs came free from Mandy. It was tiny in her hands but fully formed.

There, my child, I'm your mother now.

Isabel raised the child high in the air, as if offering it her God. She was chanting now, the words lost on Steve, the rhythm of them soothing the baby, which looked at her with wide eyes. Isabel's mouth opened wide, too far, as if her jaws were dislocating.

She brought the baby towards her face as if she was going to kiss it, but instead pushed the head into her mouth.

Steve felt sick – the element of him that was a loving father knew this was a travesty – but he was rooted to the spot.

Isabel pushed the baby into her gaping maw until it was gone, then leaned back and let out a scream that was guttural and triumphant and woke things in Steve that he'd never known were there.

At that point, what little remained of the old Steve collapsed and crawled into a dark corner of his mind, curling itself up like a cowering dog that knew it was going to be whipped.

Bring me more my familiar, many more.

Steve nodded. "As you wish, Isabel."

She came to him, her feet silent on the grass. *It has started, my familiar, and when I parade her and the others like her, this village will be made to suffer as it made me suffer.*

"What shall I do with her?"

Keep her alive, but keep her close.

"I understand."

She stroked his chin and kissed him and briefly he was lost to her.

You have done well.

"Thank you."

He watched her walk back to the memorial and disperse into smoke, filtering back into the crack in the marble.

Isabel lay in her dank cell, running her fingertips lightly over her face.

She could feel the child's energy, tingling through her decrepit blood vessels and flowering across her parchment skin. With more of this energy, she could soon rise from her tomb and confront these pathetic villagers, to show them that it didn't matter what they did, they could not consign her to the earth forever.

~

Steve carried Mandy across the beach, his steps unsteady in the shifting sands, listening to her sobbing quietly. He'd decided to put her in one of the offices in the warehouse – no-one would be there until Monday and, by then, he could get his car and take her somewhere else to hide her.

Once they were in the loading bay, Mandy seemed to realise what was happening and began to scream and wriggle. She slid out of his arms and fell onto her back on the concrete floor, her head thudding dully against it. The blow didn't stop her for long and she began to scream again, hurling accusations at him.

"Mandy, please be quiet," he said.

"Todd, you bastard. What did that fucking bitch do to me? What did you let her do to me?"

Calmly, he punched her in the face then picked her up and carried her onto the dock and past the canteen. A corridor, with half a dozen offices opening off from it, led to the warehouse. The company used the first two offices, so he went to the far end and kicked open the door of the last office.

The room smelled musty and dry and he put Mandy on the floor. He ripped off the bottom half of her dress and rolled her onto her belly, his foot in the small of her back. He tore the material into strips and tied one end around her wrists, the other around her ankles, satisfied that she had some movement but not enough to get away. He picked her up and put her against the far wall, then went out into the corridor.

All of the door handles had locks in them, which were no more effective than the lock on a toilet door, but they would serve the purpose.

He locked Mandy in, then went out to the loading dock and sat facing the sea, waiting for his breathing to return to normal.

When it had, he walked home.

CHAPTER 10

KATHY GRASPED BETH'S ARM, her small fingers pink and chubby.

They were in the orchard, sitting by a large pond that was shaded by the canopy of trees.

"I need to show you where to go, Isabel," said Kathy.

Beth looked at her cousin. "But I'm Beth, you know that."

"No," said Kathy, shaking her head slowly.

For the briefest of moments, Beth felt as if she was being roughly shaken and then she was walking along a dirt track that she didn't recognise.

~

She'd been walking for weeks, an eighteen-year-old with striking features and long red hair, whose face was full of the sorrow that she carried with her. She wasn't sure where she was heading, only certain that she had to leave the past behind.

As Beth walked into the town of Heyton, a heavily pregnant woman came out of the smithy, carrying firewood.

"Let me help you with that," she said, without thinking.

"Thank you," said the woman, gladly offering her load. "Are you heading through?"

"I am."

"But you're so young. Where is your family?"

"All gone, I am sad to say."

"You poor child," said the woman and arched, pressing her hands to the small of her back. "It's my fourth and it never seems to get easier." She smiled. "If you have nowhere to go, you could stay with us for a while. My husband and I have a farm, but I cannot do much now and I am sure he would be glad to have you. You could help out around the place and we will give you food and a roof over your head."

"That is very kind of you."

The woman laughed. "My name is Charity Astor, people say it serves me well. Come with me."

The farm was small and when they got to the cottage Beth saw a child with white blond hair sat by the front door, playing.

"My first born, John," said Charity proudly. "Sadly, he is the only one who lived."

"What happened with the others?"

Charity made a snorting sound. "According to the doctor, I do not carry well. Which is news to me, since I delivered all three. But two were dead as I birthed them."

"I am sorry."

"As am I. I have more hopes for this one," said Charity and rubbed her belly.

A man came from around the back, tall and broad-shouldered, with the same white blond hair as the boy. His shirt sleeves were rolled up to show thick, muscled arms.

"This is my husband John," said Charity.

Beth looked at John Astor and felt a peculiar fluttering in her stomach. It would be unkind to Charity, but she found herself imagining what it would feel like to be held by this man, to be kissed by him.

John put down his scythe, ruffled his child's head and waited for them.

"This waif has nowhere to say, John and carried the firewood for me. She could stay for a while, could she not, as I am of no use to you now?"

John hugged his wife and kissed to top of her head loudly. "You are always of use to me, wife of mine. Now how about dinner?"

Charity went into the house, picking her child up on the way.

Beth was aware that John was sizing her up. "Done any farm work, have you?"

"No, but I can learn."

"Good," he said and rested a hand on her behind. She felt both deliriously happy and sick at the same time. "And what is your name?"

"Isabel Mundy," she said.

~

Beth woke up and it took her a moment or two to work out where she was. The sun was bright, filling the room with a dusky light and from outside, she could hear voices and cars. It wasn't the sound of London, of people on their way to work, more the sound of people who were glad to be up and on their way to do something they would enjoy.

She looked at Rob. He was on his front, his face to her, his left arm over her chest. She stroked the top of his head and he murmured something that she didn't catch.

"I love you," she said quietly.

"Love you too," he mumbled.

Remnants of her dream came back to her, but like before, they made little sense. Why should she be dreaming she was someone else? Who was Isabel Mundy?

She shook her head to clear the remnants away and stared at the ceiling.

Her concerns, those about Rob and how their relationship would cope with the baby, were fading slowly. Back home, she'd tried to believe that they were strong enough to get through this and, after yesterday, she was sure she was right. Last night they'd made love easily and he'd explored her body as avidly as ever, paying particular attention to kissing her belly.

These thoughts were jostled away, her mind drawing back to the dream. It had to be due to stress – of losing Kathy, of becoming pregnant, perhaps even about the missing little boy.

"No," she said. Now wasn't the time to dwell on things like this – it was a sunny day, they were at the seaside and she was lying here with her lovers arm draped across her. Now was a time to reflect on all that was good.

She slid out of bed, stood up and stretched. His alarm clock read as half seven, which made her smile – she'd managed to have a lie-in. She went into the bathroom and looked at herself as she peed.

Her reflection, who recently had looked withdrawn and sometimes sad, smiled back at her. But there was still something in her eyes that said all was not right.

~

Chris Valentine opened his eyes, but the sunlight was harsh and set off a pounding in his head. He groaned and rolled over, reaching for Mandy.

His fingers patted the bedsheet and he opened his eyes again, slowly. Her side of the bed was undisturbed. He sat up, holding his head, his eyes squeezed shut against the pain.

"Mandy?" The loudness of his voice made him wince. "You here?"

There was no response so, not wanting to shout again, he got out of bed gingerly. It took him a long time to get downstairs, having checked the upstairs thoroughly and not finding her.

Post was on the doormat, all the rooms were empty, all the doors and windows locked.

He sat heavily on a kitchen stool, knowing he was stupid to worry. She wouldn't be drinking and Billy's wife-to-be couldn't hold her alcohol at the best of times, so perhaps Mandy had gone back to hers to make sure she didn't choke or swallow her tongue or do anything else equally stupid.

That made him feel better – Mandy was generally sensible and his explanation made sense. She was safe and well, sleeping soundly at the Davenports'. He could ring later, to see if she wanted him to walk around to get her, but now it seemed more important to go back upstairs and get some more sleep.

~

Beth heard movement throughout the hotel but didn't see anyone apart from two couples in the dining room, taking advantage of the speedier service. One couple was sitting at Goody June's table, but the old woman wasn't there.

Outside, Beth squinted against the bright sky and took a deep breath. The air was clean, soured only slightly by the salty scent of the sea, but much better than an Archway morning. A couple of young families walked by, the parents pushing strollers and holding the hands of excited looking children who were dressed for the beach.

She headed towards Commerce Street, the ticket for the chemist's in her shorts pocket and passed several restaurants along Marine Road that we gearing up for the day, with a few people already eating. She breathed in deeply at each one, the smell of cooking bacon and sausages making her stomach rumble.

The assistant at the chemist's was the same one as last night and he handed over her pack of photographs before she'd even given him her ticket. She paid, promised to come back if she had any more developing to do and left.

The pier was closed and it struck her how peaceful it was. There were a few kids, shouting excitedly and the odd car, but there was no loud music or screams. Deciding there was plenty of time for breakfast, she walked around a mound of bright flowers and up some steps to the walkway over the beach. The tide was out and, under the pier, a small boy was building a sand castle.

Beth sat on a bench and took the photographs out of the wallet.

"Bloody hell," she said. The film had obviously been in the camera for a long time, because the first five pictures were of last New Year, when they'd spent the evening with Bob and Theresa. Looking at the smiling faces, posing with drinks around a Pictionary board, made her smile – it had been a good night. There were some pictures of her parents, of her at Rob's flat, half a dozen of them around London and then some on The Eye, her looking worried – she'd been convinced that the wheel would tip and dump them in the Thames – and Rob looking as if he was having the time of his life.

The next picture was the one Rob had taken of the sunset and, whilst it captured some of the colours, it was dark and the chemist had put an 'under/over exposed' sticker on it.

The picture of her on the seafront was stickered as well, over her silhouette's arm.

The final picture was the one Rob had taken outside of the Slot-Time arcade and Beth felt a tingle on the back of her neck as she looked at it.

There wasn't a sticker on it, but that must have been a mistake. Something had obviously gone wrong with the development process, like the chemical reaction on the paper hadn't worked properly.

She tilted the picture but the image didn't change, the light only making the emulsion glow.

Beth felt the tingle on her neck spread across her shoulders.

Rob had been right about the picture, she did look good in front of the lights though the flash had whited out some of the detail of her face. But that wasn't the issue, nor was it the man in the nice shirt who was walking behind her in the direction of the hotel.

What was strange was that something was coming out of his back – the face of a woman, her neck joined almost at his shoulders.

Beth looked over at the kid under the pier, her eyes taking a few moments to adjust in the light, then back at the picture. When her eyes had re-adjusted, she saw that it was the same. Both she and the man were oblivious to the spectre the camera had picked up.

The woman's hair hung over her face and her eyes glared out, making her look ready to kill, her lips drawn into a tight line.

Worse than the fact that she appeared to be coming of the man's back – she'd seen enough bad pictures of people with any manner of objects 'growing' out of them – was that she obviously wasn't really there. If anything, she looked like a cloud of green smoke that Beth was somehow able to see a face in, as people often did with clouds or explosions.

Shaking her head, Beth put the pictures in her lap and took a deep breath.

When she was at school, her best friend had been obsessed with ghosts and she could remember plenty of evenings sitting in Nikki's bedroom, flicking through library books and scaring herself silly.

This, though, was different. Most ghost pictures could be explained away technically, but last night Rob had literally just pointed the camera and snapped and this woman, whoever she was, was there to be photographed. The man might have been wearing an extravagant costume, but she doubted that. If he'd been wearing anything out of the ordinary, Rob would have noticed and he hadn't said anything at all – Beth couldn't even remember seeing the passer-by.

Troubled, Beth put the photographs back in their wallet and walked back to the hotel.

～

Donna Ellis knelt beside her son's bed, her hand on his forehead. Notwithstanding last night, he was as hot as he'd ever been, his skin all clammy.

Sighing, she went to wash her hands, listening to Steve's snores coming from the lounge. He'd obviously come in late last night, pissed and hadn't been able to make it upstairs. Which was nice.

She dried her hands and looked back into Josh's room – he had rolled onto his side and kicked off his duvet. "I'll get you some water," she said and went downstairs.

The lounge door was shut and she opened it gently, one hand on the handle, the other against the frame. The smell in there was awful – farts, onions and sweat – made worse by the gloomy atmosphere with the curtains drawn.

Steve was on the sofa, fully dressed. His left arm was dangling, his fingers brushing the carpet with each breath he took and a thin trail of drool had slid over his cheek and soaked into the cushion.

"Come on, Steve," she said loudly, amazed that he could be so selfish, "time to get up."

He grunted and tried to roll over, but couldn't seem to work out that he was on the sofa and gave up quickly.

"Steve," she called, louder this time.

He grunted again, but his eyes remained steadfastly shut.

She knelt beside him and shook him. "Steve, wake up."

He swatted her hand but she kept shaking him until his eyes opened sluggishly, taking a while to focus on her. Even when they had, she didn't think he recognised her. Must have been a great night, she thought bitterly.

"What? Just leave me alone."

"Steve, come on, you stink. Get up."

"Leave me alone, or else…" he said, his tone gruff and unpleasant.

"Hey," she said, taken aback, "what's going on?" He wasn't normally an aggressive drunk – he got clumsy and ended up falling asleep usually – and she could only smell the slightest hint of alcohol on him.

"Leave me alone, woman."

"Woman?" Donna went over to the patio doors and pulled the curtains open.

Steve howled and tried to cover his face with his hands. "What'd you do that for?"

"It's time to get up, Steve. You've had your fun, now you've got to be an adult again."

"Fuck off and leave me alone."

His words stopped her dead and she could feel the surprise in her every pore. "What did you say?"

Unsteadily, he sat up. "I warned you, woman. Now just leave me the fuck alone."

Her anger, coupled with tiredness and stress, flared. "Who the hell do you think you're talking to? I was up most of last night, trying to keep Josh cool and you go out and get smashed and then start this? Just who the fuck do you think…"

He stood up suddenly, swaying on his feet. "I'm not drunk, for your information. I'm just tired."

She couldn't stop her voice from rising. "And you don't think I am?"

"Shut it, woman, I've had enough."

"Oh right," she said, giving in to her anger, "fine. Get out of here and don't come back until you're ready to be civil."

He was rotating his head slowly and he looked at her with his chin almost on his chest, a smirk at his lips. "That might be never."

"Then fuck off all the same. See if I care."

"If that's what you wish," he said, cocking his head.

"What the hell's gotten into you, Steve?"

"I don't know," he said, that same smirk intact, "but I like it."

"Get out," she screamed and crossed the room, trying to bundle him out of the door, "get out, get out, get out."

"I'm going," he said and opened the front door.

"Don't come back like this, you hear me?"

If he did, he showed no sign of it and she heard him get into the car and rev the engine. "That's right," she shouted, "break the car" and then he was skidding out of the driveway.

She watched until the car was out of sight, her heart thumping, unable to believe what had just happened. She stepped back through the door and heard Josh crying.

"Mummy's coming," she called and ran up the stairs.

~

Beth met Rosie as she crossed the driveway of the Clairmont.

"Good morning, Rosie, how are you?"

"I'm fine, my dear," she said and squinted at Beth. "Better than you, anyway. What's the matter?"

"Nothing," said Beth, forcing a smile.

Rosie pursed her lips. "Hmmm, if you say so." She touched Beth's arm. "I'm glad I caught you though."

"Why?"

"I wanted to tell you to take care. I can feel that dark cloud getting stronger, the darkness is gathering."

"What do you mean?"

Rosie laughed, without humour. "Listen to me, an old woman rambling on."

"No, what did you mean about the dark cloud and the darkness gathering?"

"I'm a silly old woman sometimes, Beth, and I have no right to scare you."

"Tell me, please."

"No, I shouldn't scare you when you're on holiday." Rosie patted her arm and began to hobble away, towards the pavement. Beth watched her go, feeling scared and stupid – scared at what the old woman meant, if anything and stupid, because all of this, all of these signs, could be nothing more than some grand coincidence that she was reading far too much into.

Rosie stopped at the edge of the driveway and turned around. "Please take care of yourself, Beth."

"I will," she said, "and you do too."

Beth watched her go and then went into the hotel, studiously not looking into the dining room just in case Goody June was in there.

As she walked upstairs, Beth's mind was a flurry of activity. Was any of this really happening – seeing Kathy, dreaming about her and someone called Isabel, Rosie and her predictions, the photograph – or was it all some kind of stress-induced hallucination? Would she wake up in her own bed, thankful that it had just been a dream?

She checked the picture again. It wasn't a dream. But what was she going to do about it? If she showed it to Rob – and he actually saw the woman, forcing Beth to question her whole state of mind, if not her sanity – he would come up with some kind of rational explanation and that would be it. If she pressed the issue, he might ask her what else was troubling her and then what? If he didn't understand her 'episodes', how could she expect him to believe everything else?

Beth stopped on the landing and decided not to show him the photograph. She put it into her handbag and walked to their room.

Rob was in the shower, the bathroom door closed, so she sat on the bed and flicked through the photographs again. She concentrated on the ones from Bob and Theresa's – a really good evening, from when things were healthy on the employment front, she wasn't pregnant and Kathy wasn't dead. A time of life where the worries they had had were now long forgotten.

Rob came out of the bathroom, rubbing his head with a towel. "Hello gorgeous," he said and leaned down to kiss her. "Hey, you got the pictures."

She watched him pull on a pair of boxers. "Sure did," she said and passed the pictures to him.

He flicked through the photographs, as surprised as she'd been at how old some of them were. He came to the ones from the sea-front – "you see, I can lighten those up a treat" – and then he was back to New Year.

"That's odd, I thought I took one of you outside the arcade."

Beth shrugged. "The camera wound the film back, maybe it didn't come out properly."

He nodded. "Could be, but that's a shame because you looked good." He got up and found some socks. "Is the dining room open still?"

Beth remembered that she was hungry. "I hope so, I was waiting for you."

"Bugger," he said and rooted around in his rucksack for a T-shirt, "better get a shift on then."

~

The dining room was almost full now and Beth picked a table by the windows, well away from Goody June's place, though she didn't seem to be there.

"That was lovely," said Rob, when he'd finished.

"I don't think I could eat another thing," Beth said, putting her knife and fork down.

"Well seeing as we're both stuffed, why don't we take it easy today and just hit the beach? Perhaps we can get a bit of sun, so that I don't look like a complete pasty gonk when I get back."

Beth drank some of her strong tea. "Okay, sounds good."

CHAPTER 11

THERE WERE MORE PEOPLE about now and Beth looked at those she passed, wondering if she'd seen any of them this morning. Were they still having a nice day, as she'd been until she picked up the photographs?

Rob took her hand and they crossed Marine Road, heading towards the fair, which was in full swing, the air filled with the sound of children screaming with pleasure.

"Let's cut through the park behind the fair," Rob suggested.

Beth looked at him, the sun shining on his face. He looked so handsome, like he would protect her forever. "Sounds good."

A group of children had blocked the pavement, standing in front of the log flume trying to get themselves soaked. Beth led the way around them and passed the slatted fence of the fair.

She stopped outside the park. "This looks nice," she said, "I wonder what it's called?"

Rob shrugged. "Don't know. Maybe the locals call it something and us out-of-towners aren't ever supposed to find out."

There were a lot of people in the park, with several young families dotted across the grass, parents looking on as chubby children took faltering steps before, invariably, falling over. There were perhaps a dozen teenagers, some reading on their own, some listening to music and apparently asleep and others cuddling up to their lovers, picking grass and talking.

From here, Beth could hear the fair – the machinery and music and screams – but the park seemed above that, content to be quiet. She stepped onto the grass, which was surprisingly soft and springy, and frowned at some tyre marks, feeling something nagging gently in the back of her mind.

~

In her dank cell, Isabel stirred as something above ground resonated within it.

There were a lot of people up there. She was aware of their presence, but none of them presented either a threat or a treat. Except for the woman.

She'd seen her through Steve briefly last night and had been captured on the device the woman's companion used. She'd become aware of that this morning, the woman sitting near the beach and looking at the image of Isabel, wondering what it was.

The woman could see. Not everything and in nowhere near as much depth as would make her a true witch, but she had the gift and that was dangerous to Isabel now. Also, unluckily for her, she was with child.

Isabel felt a sudden hatred for the woman and wanted her to suffer, to deny her the child she was carrying. It might be fun to play with her a little while beforehand, before she took great delight in removing her baby.

~

Beth stood in front of the memorial.

"Why would a six-foot spike commemorate lost sailors? Shouldn't it be a cross?"

Rob was kneeling down, reading from a tablet of names. "It looks like it's been here a long time, perhaps the people who put it up were godless."

"It's not that old," she scoffed.

"Don't discount the witches, they were big around here once. Maybe Matthew Hopkins wasn't quick enough to stop them from putting up a spike rather than a cross."

"Witches? You're an idiot." She tapped the top of his head. "Come on, the beach is calling."

"Did you pick up my camera?"

"No, why?"

"Bugger, I'd forget my head if it wasn't screwed on. Do you want to wait here and I'll go back and get it?"

The hotel wasn't far, but she quite fancied the idea of sitting here on her own for a bit, taking advantage of the peace and quiet. "Just make sure you run."

Rob gestured towards the sun. "Like that's going to happen."

"Don't keep me waiting," she said and kissed him quickly. He grinned at her and walked away. "Run," she said and he obliged her by speeding up his pace slightly.

Beth sat on one of the benches that lined the fence separating the park from the fair and rubbed her belly gently, leaning her head back and basking in the sun.

She felt the soft buzzing, rather than heard it and opened her eyes expecting to see an aeroplane, but the sky was completely clear. The buzzing got louder and the hairs on her forearms prickled. She rubbed them briskly and looked around. Perhaps something in the fair was vibrating against the fence and through the bench?

Beth stood up and the buzzing got louder. Then the images hit her like a ton of bricks.

She was in some woods, not the same as the orchard from her dream and she was being pursued. She couldn't see the people, but she could hear them and their angry cries.

Then she was in water. She tried to get up, but hands were pining her down and the cold water lapped over her face. She tried to scream and water ran down her throat.

Beth opened her eyes with a start and looked around quickly, but no-one was near her and the buzzing had stopped. Her throat was dry and she felt a cold sweat on her forehead.

Had that been another episode? If so, what on earth could it mean? And why? She couldn't remember ever having had so many in such a short space of time – how stressed could she possibly be? Or was she going slowly mad, the episodes an outward sign of her impending mental collapse?

No, she wasn't going mad, she just needed a little while longer to chill out. Her London self had felt smothered, in the middle of it, whilst out here, with the ability to relax, it had all piled on top of her. Perhaps it was a good thing. She could work her way through it, try to figure out what was going on and then maybe arrange to see her doctor when she got back, to see if she could suggest some way to help herself.

She saw Rob come around the corner. He waved and she waved back and went to meet him, not wanting him to suspect for even a moment that there was something wrong.

$\sim$

'Flo's Diner' was just outside of Heyton and Steve pulled in when he realised that his stomach ached because he was hungry. He'd spent the morning driving around aimlessly, not quite sure of why he was in his car or why he couldn't go home.

He went inside and found a seat by the window, looking out at the cars flashing by on the road, filled with people who knew what they were doing and where they were going.

He ordered an All-Day breakfast and the service was fast, the food as good as he remembered it from when he'd brought Josh in once for a treat, when Heyton Town had almost progressed to the fourth round of the FA Vase.

As he finished his meal, with indigestion burning in his chest, he watched a car pull up in the car park. A man and two young children got out and he shepherded them towards the restaurant entrance, putting himself between them and the road.

What had happened at home? Things there seemed to be seriously damaged and he didn't know how to repair them. Something swam in the back of his mind, just out of his grasp, to do with The Yard but its meaning escaped him.

The waitress came over and refilled his mug of tea.

~

The park was bordered by a dry-stone wall that had a gap in it, for some steps down to the beach.

On the soft, warm sand, Beth looked around with her hand shielding her eyes. To her right, large rocks had been wedged against the embankment, a sign proclaiming them part of the 'Heyton Coastal Defence Project'. To her left the beach stretched out, golden in the morning sun, towards the pier, where the rides were now operating.

"It's quiet here," said Rob.

The nearest person was a hundred yards or more away, with most of the sunbathers gathered near to the pier. "We could be on a desert island, couldn't we?"

The rollercoaster rumbled behind them and somebody screamed. Rob laughed. "Apart from that, of course."

He set off, his feet sinking in the loose sand and giving him a peculiar gait that made Beth smile. She kicked off her trainers, picked them up and followed him. The sand caught her out too, shifting under her feet and when he turned around, he laughed at her. She stuck two fingers up at him.

He stopped fifty yards from the steps, at the top of a hump in the beach. There was no kelp or driftwood nearby, so they probably wouldn't have to worry about moving when the tide came in.

Beth sat on the towel he'd laid out and brushed sand off the soles of her feet.

"The sun's really hot, isn't it?" he said, looking out to sea.

"And to think you wanted to go to Barbados."

He smiled at her. "I'm a fool, what can I say?"

"That's about as much as you can say," she said and pulled her T-shirt over her head. She folded it and adjusted the straps of her bikini top. "Aren't you going to get bored sitting here all day?"

"Are you mad, woman? How could I get bored looking at those boobs all day?"

"You charmer." She licked her lower lip, seductively. "So did you want to rub some cream on me?"

"Oh yes," he said and got it out of the bag, then knelt on his towel and squirted some in his hand.

She laid flat and closed her eyes against the sun as he rubbed the cream in, his hands moving in smooth, pressured strokes. The feeling, with the heat on her skin, his touch and the coolness of the cream, was very pleasant and she murmured her approval.

"Are you enjoying this?" he said and started on her legs.

"Aren't you?"

"Absolutely," he said and groaned. "Damn, I've finished."

"Did you want me to do you?"

"What here?" he said, feigning offence. "Ms Hammond, what kind of man do you take me for?"

"Fair enough," she said and shifted to a more comfortable position. "Your loss."

She listened as he put the cream on himself and then settled next to her, his hand searching for hers. She grasped it tightly, glad to feel him there.

~

By midday, Steve was on his third mug of tea and the waitress was looking at him as if she expected him to order something else.

He wasn't hungry though and was content sitting by the window. He felt safe here, surrounded by people he didn't know. He'd found a newspaper when he went to the toilet and had done the sports crossword and attempted the cryptic. He was glad for the mental exercise, to stop his thoughts from churning around and around and not getting anywhere.

Steve?

He turned and saw Isabel walking down the narrow corridor that led to the toilets. She was naked, her red hair flowing behind her, her feet tapping lightly on the lino. Surprised, he glanced around but no-one else seemed able to see her. The waitress was looking at him and he signalled for her to come over.

"Yes, love?"

"Can you get me another breakfast?" he said.

Isabel snaked behind the waitress and slid into the seat across from him. She smiled and drummed her fingertips lightly on the tabletop.

"Is that all?" asked the waitress.

He nodded and waited for her to look at Isabel, to find out what she wanted. But she didn't, she just nodded, put her pad into her smock and walked away.

Hello.

She leaned forward and rested her chin in her hands. He couldn't tear his gaze from her eyes and everything suddenly seemed right in his world – he didn't need Donna, he didn't need to worry about anything. All that mattered to him, all that would ever matter, was sitting across from him.

You still have tasks, my familiar. You must go back to Heyton tonight, to continue what you started.

"What happened last night? I can't remember anything."

She smiled. *You will. When you have completed your tasks, you and I can be together like we were before. You enjoyed that, didn't you?*

"Yes," he said. Remembering the dream gave him an erection.

From now on, you will only know of your role for me. And soon…

106

She leaned forward, propped on her elbows and he watched her nipples graze the edge of the table.

...soon we can be together forever.

She was right in front of him now.

"Yes," he said and they kissed.

Before, he'd been convinced she was an hallucination – what else would explain the waitress being unable to see her – but that wasn't the case. Her lips, pressed to his, were firm and supple and her hand, holding the back of his neck, had a firm grip. Her touch was like nothing he'd ever felt before and he wanted her right there, at that moment and damn the consequences.

She drew back and he leaned forward, trying to keep the contact.

No.

"But I want you, Isabel."

And you will, when you have completed your task.

"But how can I complete it? How will I know who is suitable?"

Isabel ran the backs of her fingers down his cheeks. *Now you will know.*

There was a clatter to his side and he looked up, as if waking from a dream, as the waitress put his breakfast on the table.

"That all?" she asked.

"Yes," he said, wanting her to go away, "thank you."

The waitress nodded and left. Steve looked over, but Isabel had gone.

That caused a weird pang of hurt, deep in his belly, but it seemed to clear his mind perfectly. Gone was the lack of direction, gone were the thoughts of home and what could be done about the situation there, gone even were thoughts of Josh and how he was doing.

He would drive back to Heyton, find some women there and deliver them to Isabel. It was all so simple.

~

Beth rolled onto her side, resting her chin on Rob's arm.

"Hey gorgeous," he said. "You finish your book?"

"I did."

He reached over and held the cover so that he could see it. "'All That Mullarkey'?" he said. "Chick-Lit, eh?" He didn't like Chick-Lit very much.

"It's a good book."

"I'm sure it is."

"Mr Sarky. And there I was, going to be nice and ask if you still wanted to see 'Rear Window' tonight?"

He looked at his watch. "If you're sure."

"Like I said, we're on holiday. And it's been ages since I last saw it, all I can remember is the view out of the window."

"We ought to make a move then, if we're going to get sorted out and fed before the film."

She rubbed a trickle of sweat off her cheek. "I think we've sunned ourselves enough, don't you?"

He stroked her belly and held up his hand, his fingers dripping a mixture of melted sun-cream and sweat. "I think so," he said and flicked his fingers at the sand.

~

Chris Valentine slept until 5pm and woke up feeling like he'd gone ten rounds with a heavyweight boxer.

He sat up and listened for Mandy, but the house was silent. If she was in, she'd be singing or he'd be able to hear the radio or TV. His stomach panged with worry and he reached for the phone, ringing Billy's number from memory.

"Hi, Carla, it's Chris. How're you?"

"Rough. Drank too much last night, that's a fact."

He tried to laugh, but failed. "Last chance before you're chained to Billy for the rest of your natural."

That made Carla bray with laughter. He winced and held the receiver away from his ear. When she was done, he said, "Is Mandy there?"

"Nope, haven't seen her. She went off to get the drinks before the fight started and we didn't see her again."

"What do you mean?"

Carla spoke slowly, as if Chris was stupid. "She went home, Allie saw her go off."

"What time was that?"

"Dunno, about one-ish. Isn't she there then?"

"She didn't come home last night."

"No." There was a pause, as Carla took the news in. "Really?"

"Really," said Chris and listened, with decreasing attention, as Carla wittered on about what might have happened and how she would get in touch with Allie to find out if Mandy had left with anyone, though she doubted that, since Mandy was very happy with her lot in life.

He put the phone down on her without saying anything else, more worried than ever. There was no reason for her not to come home – as Carla had said, she was happy with her lot in life, especially with the baby coming.

He rang directory enquiries and got the number for Heyton Police Station. He'd lived on the coast long enough to know that people could go missing very easily and he didn't want Mandy to become one of those statistics.

CHAPTER 12

BETH SPEARED A CHUNK of sausage and chewed it thoughtfully, watching Rob eat his like he hadn't had a square meal in a long time.

They'd showered before coming down for dinner, where the set meal was sausage and chips, which suited them both. As they started to eat, the cuckoo clock chimed for six thirty.

She didn't realise that her mind had wandered until Rob's voice cut through her thoughts. "Beth?" She looked up, surprised. "Are you okay?"

No, she thought. I keep seeing things that aren't there, I'm worried about the baby and what it might do to us and I'm having strange dreams.

She smiled and hoped her face didn't betray the lie. "I think so."

"You looked like you were miles away."

"No, I'm right here."

He looked at her without speaking and, self-conscious, she wiped her mouth and he laughed.

"What?"

"Nothing," he said, "I was just looking at you, trying to take in how beautiful you were."

"Me? Beautiful?"

"Yes and you know it," he said, smiling as he speared another piece of sausage and some chips.

Beth smiled and looked around the room. Most of the tables were occupied by now and, even though she didn't really want to, she looked towards the kitchen, but Goody June wasn't there. She frowned and looked around again – Rosie wasn't in here either. She hoped the old woman was okay.

~

After eating, they took a slow wander to the cinema. The evening air was warm and she led the way, holding Rob's hand tightly.

"Isn't this all glorious?" he said.

111

CONJURE

"It's the perfect end to a lovely day."

He didn't so anything and the atmosphere between them suddenly seemed to chill. She looked into an arcade, hoping and praying that he wouldn't say what she thought he would.

But he did. "So what's wrong then?"

"Eh?" she said, forcing herself to concentrate on the pavement rather than look at him.

"Come on, Beth, I'm not a fool. Something's wrong, I can see it. Is it something that I've done?"

"No," she said, turning to him and walking sideways, not having realised he might think it was his fault. She had to make him believe that he'd got the wrong end of the stick because, however ill at ease she felt, she knew it'd be a lot worse if Rob wasn't by her side. "Really, it's not you."

"Then what is it?"

She took a deep breath. Was now the right time to tell him everything – about her dreams and what had happened to her in the park? Was it the right time to show him the photograph? But what if all of this wasn't real, that it was some kind of mental deterioration brought on by stress and hormones and fear for the future? If that was the case, there might not ever be a right time to say anything and she felt the tug of contradiction.

Beth shook her head. "Just the same kind of stuff as always, you know? Kathy, work." She ran a hand gently across her belly. "Junior. Same old, same old."

He stopped and tugged her hand, making her stop too and pulled her close to him. "I can't do much about the same old, same old, can I?"

She forced a smile. "Probably not, it's all in my head."

"Some of it might be," he nodded, "but not everything. I can't help everything but I can do something about Junior, I can do something about making you happy."

"You do make me happy, Rob, really you do."

He kissed her and started to walk again. "Good. Because you make me happier than I've ever been, Beth Hammond, you really do."

His words warmed her, made her feel better and she walked with him, content in their closeness, not letting her mind wander past the present moment, not now.

~

Driving in town on Saturday nights during high season was a nightmare and Steve tried to avoid it as often as possible. But he needed to be here now so he gritted his teeth and kept a watch out for people on either side of Marine Road who might lurch out in front of him without warning.

The car in front of him slowed down, as they crawled towards a crossing. As the green man lit up, a crowd surged into the road, all in their late teens or early twenties, dressed for a night out and most of them already half-cut. He watched them, uninterested even by the amount of skin the women were showing, until one caught his attention.

She was in the middle of the crowd, wearing a yellow bra-top and a pale green mini-skirt that didn't hide a lot. Her legs were pale and thick and she was walking slightly stooped forward, as if either her skirt or heels were restricting movement. He didn't really see any of that, all he could focus on was the strip of her bare belly showing between her bra-top and skirt.

Ordinarily, he might not have paid much attention to what he saw, dismissing it as a trick of the light, but tonight, for some reason, he knew it wasn't.

She had a glow.

It started just below her breasts, a faint orange glow that blanketed her stomach. He stared hard at it, trying to work out what it was and then she rubbed her belly lightly with her hand, just below her belly button and he knew.

It was something that Donna had done, that he'd seen hundreds of other women do.

She was pregnant. Was this what Isabel had meant in the diner, when she'd touched his cheek?

A horn sounded behind him, making him jump. The crowd was on the path now, moving towards the pier, the girl lost to him. He waved to the driver behind and drove away, scanning the pavements for more glows.

They were everywhere and he couldn't believe his luck. A couple were standing in the queue at the Empire, the man looking at the poster for a Hitchcock film, the girl looking in her handbag, her belly glowing. A girl came out of the arcade next to the cinema, glowing. More were walking along, some with partners, others with girlfriends or in crowds, clearly glowing with pregnancy.

A heavily pregnant woman came out of the Slot-Time arcade, her glow the same colour as the others.

"Thank you, Isabel," he said and smiled.

~

There was a small queue outside the cinema, which surprised Rob, but they joined the end of it. He looked up at the old building, standing tall and proud, squashed between a one-storey pub that stretched back to a three-storey hotel and an amusement arcade.

The Empire was a relic from a different era, the gaping maw of the entrance flanked by four pillars on two sides, all of them intricately carved from stone. On the second floor, three windows with ornate arches opened out onto a small, stone balcony. The current Empire sign was neon, crackling in the evening light, but the old tiled lettering was still clearly visible beneath it.

"They don't make them like this any more, do they?" he said.

"Nope." She rubbed his arm briskly. "So are you looking forward to this?"

"I am," he said and he was. Partly it was because this cinema looked as if it was a labour of love, but mostly because he didn't like multiplexes – they felt cold to him and impersonal. He enjoyed the experience of a small venue, with counter staff who knew what they were talking about, in a building that was a temple to flickering light and designed to take people away from their lives briefly, rather than just rob them of money, sitting with others who felt the same way about film as he did.

He'd taken Beth to an arts cinema once, but it wasn't a success.

"If there are subtitles, you spend more time reading them than watching the damned film," she'd told him, after sitting and apparently suffering through a French film that he'd loved. He knew it was a valid argument and didn't press the point.

Tonight, for him, was the icing on the cake. It had been a great day and now he was going to watch a Hitchcock film on the big screen at last. When he'd heard the draw result, he'd been convinced the holiday was going to be awful but he'd been wrong. They'd had a nice time so far and he still had the big surprise to spring on Beth.

The queue moved them to the front steps, where a newspaper board had been set up, with some 'Rear Window' one-sheets on it.

Yes, he decided, this was going to be a great night.

~

Steve walked down the office corridor, a torch in one hand – though there was still enough light from outside to see – a bottle of water and a pack of sandwiches in the other.

Mandy had started shouted as soon as he opened the door. "Help! You have to help me, I've been locked in here. Help me!"

He smiled, tapping the bottle-top on the wall as he walked.

"I'm down here. Please, you have to help me."

He reached her door. "Are you hurt?"

She screamed, a mixture of surprise and relief. "No," she cried, "I don't think so. I can't believe you're here, I've been calling for ages. Come on, quick, you have to get me out of here."

He unlocked the door and pushed it open, shining the torch where he remembered putting her down. She wasn't there anymore and he played the torch beam along the floor, following a glistening trail on the concrete. She'd moved herself across the room, but had stayed against the back wall.

Mandy was crouched in the corner, almost kneeling so that her bindings were loose. She closed her eyes against the beam and brought her hands up as far as they would go, to offer more protection.

"You pissed yourself," he said.

"I couldn't help it," she said, her voice hoarse, "I've been in here for ages. You have to get me out, I'm pregnant and I don't want my baby to be harmed."

He frowned. Why wasn't she a gibbering wreck? Couldn't she remember what Isabel had done to her, surely it had imprinted on her mind? Or had she blanked it out altogether, unable to properly deal with it?

"How long have you been in here?"

She lowered her hands and squinted at the light. "I don't know, there's no window. It was Friday night, what day is it today?"

"Saturday," he said quietly.

"Oh my God, I've been in here a day? Is it light outside, or dark? Come on, get me untied, you have to get me out of here."

"Sorry, Mandy, I can't do that."

At the mention of her name, she opened her eyes wide. They were bloodshot, as if she'd been crying a lot. "Todd?"

"Uh huh, so I can't rescue you really. I've just called by with some food and drink, I don't want you dying on me."

"You fucking arsehole, just get me out of here."

He pursed his lips, shaking his head at her attitude. "I got you the breakfast sarnie, with bacon and egg and sausage. I thought you'd be hungry."

"I don't want feeding, you stupid bastard, I want to get out of here."

"Sorry, can't do that," he said and walked towards her, keeping the torch beam on her face. He knelt in front of her and put the bottle and sandwich pack by her leg. She looked towards the sound with a look of utter desperation on her face.

"It smells in here," he said and she spat at him.

He wiped her saliva away with his sleeve and went out into the corridor, locking the door behind him and ignoring her screamed threats and curses.

～

Inside the reception of the Empire, there was a small ticket machine beside the staircase and a chirpy looking, thick-set woman, sat behind it, her uniform fighting a losing battle to stay together at the seams. She smiled brightly at Rob.

"Two?" she asked. "Circle or stalls?"

"Two for the circle, please," he said and handed over his five pounds.

The woman pressed a button twice, two tickets spitting out of the metallic mouth on the counter in front of her. She handed them to Rob. "Go up the steps here," she said, leaning back and pointing to her left, "and Maurice will guide you to your seats."

"Thank you," said Rob and he followed Beth towards the staircase.

When they were a few yards away, Beth leaned back to him and he felt her breath on his neck. "How old fashioned is this?" she said quietly.

"I love it," he said and led her up the thickly carpeted steps to the first-level landing. The place was almost gothic – the ceilings were very high, with ornate cornices and a large chandelier and the banister was elaborately carved from a dark wood. Even better, it was obviously past its prime – the carpet pattern was rubbing off with the heavy tread of patrons, the plaster on the walls and ceiling was starting to crack and the whole place had a wonderful air of decayed elegance.

A pair of velvet curtains faced them, pulled aside to reveal a heavy door. A thin man stood next to it, wearing a red and black suit that had seen better days, a name-tag on his left breast indicating his name was Maurice.

"Good evening," he said, "do you have your tickets?"

Rob handed them over and Maurice read them quickly.

"Follow me, please," he said and led them through the door and up half a dozen steps before indicating with his torch beam the seats they were supposed to take. Beth sat down, leaving Rob the aisle seat so that he could stretch his legs.

"Enjoy the film," said Maurice and walked away.

The auditorium was lit by three chandeliers, one above their heads, one over the stalls and one above the riser in front of the screen. Even with that, it seemed dark and snug, the furnishings brown or deep reds, the theatre shaped like a lozenge. The balcony wall, six rows in front of them, hid any people who might have been sitting in the stalls but the bottom edge of the screen – from where Rob sat – was at least a foot above it.

"How cool is this place?" he said.

"It's different from the Odeon, that's a fact."

He leaned back in his chair and put his arm around Beth and she snuggled into his shoulder.

"I love you, you know," he said.

"And I love you too."

"Good," he said.

~

117

CONJURE

As he got into his car, Steve knew that he was going to have to be careful finding the women for Isabel. He would have to cast his net wider than the strip, for starters, so as not to draw attention to himself. With hindsight, Mandy Valentine wasn't the best candidate he could have chosen, but that was done now and he would have to figure out somewhere to put her.

He decided to try the holiday camp at the other end of Marine Road. He drove past the pier, to the quiet stretch where the houses were exclusive and set well away from the road, hidden from prying eyes by hedges, conifers and walls.

Eight hundred yards from the pier was The Happy Cow, the last café before the road curved up towards the holiday camp and then round towards the docks.

A tall, dark haired woman, wearing a halter top and a skirt that almost touched her ankles, was standing outside of the café, arguing with a man. He was against the café wall, between her and the menu board and she was in his face, shouting something that Steve couldn't make out.

Her belly was glowing.

Steve watched them in his rear view mirror as he pulled up across the road. The man shoved her shoulder, knocking her off balance and she staggered back a couple of steps, clearly surprised. The man shouted at her and stalked off, heading for the pier. The woman stared after him and then shouted something. He held his hand up and gave her the finger.

"Perfect," said Steve and he did a U-turn and parked at the kerb.

When the man reached the pier, he turned and flipped the girl the bird again, before walking out of sight behind the theatre complex.

Steve got out of the car and sauntered over to the woman, who was leaning against the wall as if intently studying the menu. The movement of her shoulders gave away that she was crying.

He stood next to her. "Hey, are you okay?"

"I'm fine, just leave me alone please, yeah?"

It took him a moment or two to place her accent as West Country, probably Bristol. She was a long way from home.

"Are you hurt?"

She stood up straight, her tear stained face angry. "Just piss off and leave me alone, alright?"

He shoved her against the wall and pushed her along a little way, her back skidding against the brickwork, the anger draining from her face.

He grabbed her shoulders and leaned in close, his face inches from hers. "You're not very polite, are you?"

The woman looked terrified and clearly didn't have a clue as to what was going on or how she should react to it. "What do you want?" she managed to stammer out.

"You, in my car, now. Nice and quiet and easy. You aren't going to get raped or killed, but I will hit you if I have to, it doesn't make a bit of difference to me."

"In your car?"

"Yes. Nice and quiet and easy, remember?"

"Okay," she said finally, nodding her head. "I remember." She took a deep breath and screamed for help.

"Shit." He punched her, bending forward so that she fell over his shoulder.

As he walked by the entrance to The Happy Cow, a man came out to see what the commotion was.

"Too much to drink," said Steve, as he folded the woman into the passenger seat and strapped her in. "I don't know what it is about girls and drink."

The man, who'd managed to ignore the shouted argument and the woman's heartfelt shriek for help until it was too late, shook his head at the stupidity of strangers and went back into the café.

Steve got into the car and turned the engine on. Away from prying eyes, he would stick this woman in the boot, try to find another target and take them both back to The Yard.

The woman moaned, pushing against the seatbelt and Steve drove away.

He was sure Isabel would be happy with his plan.

CHAPTER 13

THE LIGHTS SLOWLY DIMMED and the sound of a pipe organ filled the auditorium.

"I wonder if an organist has popped up?" said Beth.

"I doubt it," said Rob, but he stood up to make sure.

The music faded, the curtains drew back from the screen and the projector whirred, noisily, into life. Beams of light pierced the darkness above them and an animated logo for the Empire burst onto the screen. It was followed by a set of cubes, racing towards them.

"My God," said Rob, "it's Pearl & Dean."

Ten minutes of adverts for local shops, restaurants and amusements played, each one cheesier than the last, until finally the screen went dark.

"Good evening, ladies and gentlemen," boomed a voice that made Beth jump. It sounded like Maurice, trying to emulate voice-over man from rental videos. "Welcome to the Heyton Empire. Ahead of tonight's screening of Alfred Hitchcock's 'Rear Window', we are pleased to announce that we will be showing the theatrical trailers for both this film and 'Psycho'. We hope you enjoy the show."

"Brilliant," said Rob, "this just gets better."

Beth had felt some pressure on her bladder since coming into the cinema and decided to go now, before the film started. She leaned close to Rob and told him.

"Just watch your step in the dark, won't you?"

"I'll be fine. See you in a minute."

Beth ducked her head as she went down the steps, as Alfred Hitchcock loomed big on the screen and told his audience about a 'quiet little motel'.

Maurice held the door open for her and she went through the velvet curtains, blinking in the sudden glare of light. The sun was shining through the picture windows above the main entrance, making the landing carpet glow.

Above the door, an arrow pointed to each staircase off the landing, labelled 'toilets'.

She went up the stairs to her right and it curved left, the picture windows giving her a bird's eye view of the theatre complex and pier. The stairs opened onto another landing, a high railing making it a balcony to look down over the foyer.

A door in the wall was marked 'Projection Room – No Admittance'. To its left was the door marked 'Toilets', which onto a narrow corridor that led to the ladies.

The ladies' toilet shared the same gothic splendour as the rest of the cinema. A large room, it had five cubicles against the wall to her left, a bank of five sinks across from her and a mirror that stretched all the way across the wall above them. The tiled walls were racing green to the midpoint and cream to the high ceiling. On the wall to her left were large framed prints of the Hollywood Greats – she recognised Jean Harlow, Carole Lombard and Greta Garbo, but not the other two. Three domed fittings on the ceiling filled the room with glaring white light.

"Impressive," she said to her reflection and went into the middle cubicle, her shoes clacking against the tiled floor.

The toilet was old fashioned, with a high cistern and a metal-link chain for the flush and very clean. Beth got the feeling it wasn't a deliberately retro-look, but just the way it had always been. From somewhere, she could hear a steady drip and its slight echo from another cistern.

She wiped the seat with some toilet paper, pulled her jeans and panties down and sat on the cold wooden seat.

The door opened and someone came in, wearing high heels, the tips clacking loudly against the tiles. The door shushed closed as a tap ran.

"Jesus," sighed the newcomer.

There was a pattering sound, which Beth assumed was the woman flicking excess water from her hands and the towel holder pulled twice.

"What am I going to do?" the woman asked as her heels telegraphed her progress out the door, which shushed gently shut behind her.

Beth felt uncomfortable, like a voyeur. The woman had sounded unhappy and thought she was alone – but then, who went into a toilet and checked for feet under cubicle doors?

The only sound in the toilet now was the steady, echoing drip.

The door shushed again. She heard no footsteps and assumed it was someone using the gents, the draught of that door causing the ladies one to open slightly.

Something pattered against the floor.

Beth sat up, not exactly worried, but concerned that someone would come in and keep quiet. There was another patter and then silence.

Beth shook her head – it must have been her imagination. After the things she'd seen and felt the last couple of days, it wouldn't surprise her if she'd confused a dripping tap with the sound of something pattering on the floor.

There was a slap and it took Beth a moment to recognise the sound as being like a swimmer, coming out of a pool and walking along. She frowned. Why would someone come up three flights of stairs barefoot to use a toilet? And wouldn't their feet have dried on the carpet?

The slaps of the bare feet were as clear as the sighing woman's heels, giving Beth the mental image of someone going to the sinks.

Panic started to nag at her as she strained to hear anything other than the damp footsteps, but there was no breathing or water being run from the taps, no cubicle doors closing. The panic wasn't so much that someone was in here, more that they were being quiet. She had the horrible feeling that no-one else was on this floor, that nobody would come running should she need to scream.

That unnerved her and she decided the best thing to do would be to get out of the toilet quickly. If someone was out there, she could do with it, but in here, she was just scaring herself.

She wiped and got dressed as quietly as she could. Before she pulled the chain, she paused but could only hear the same steady dripping.

Cautiously – and feeling a little paranoid and silly – she unlatched the door and peered around. She saw herself in the mirror, the two cubicles on either side of her but nobody in front of them or at the sinks. Or by the main door.

Rather than alleviate the panic, the realisation that she was alone made it nag harder and she cast her mind back, trying to figure out just what she'd heard. Could it have been a trick of the acoustics, with all the tiles, or perhaps leakage from the cinema below?

But what about the shushing door?

No, someone had definitely come in here and not left. So where were they?

Beth pulled the chain, the sound of the flush incredibly loud. She left the cubicle, looking left and right and went to the sink.

She could now see all five cubicles, the doorway and the fact that the fifth cubicle was butted to the wall. There was a ten-inch gap below the cubicle doors and she couldn't see any feet or signs of movement, no wet footprints visible anywhere.

That settled it for her, it had to have been some kind of aural hallucination.

She breathed a sigh of relief and turned on the tap. Any kind of hallucination – aural or visual – wasn't good, especially after everything that had happened over the past few days, but at least she was safe here.

She pumped soap into her palms and looked at herself in the mirror. The light in here was unforgiving, made brighter by the tiles and this close, she did look tired and stressed. She'd heard – and witnessed it with women at work – that pregnancy made the mother-to-be shine, made her hair thicker and glossier and her skin healthier looking. It hadn't worked for her yet – her eyes were dark against her pale skin, even with the glow from the sun this afternoon.

She looked down and rinsed her hands, then looked back into the mirror and gasped, her sharp intake of breath echoing. Though against what, she couldn't tell.

Everything behind her was gone. The mirrors and sink were still there, but the cubicles and ceiling, the walls and the floor, weren't.

She was in a clearing, in a wood, looking at a pool.

The light was dusky, the sky filled with dark, angry clouds, flashes of lightning visible in them. The trees around the pool were autumnal, the almost bare branches waving in the rough wind that she could hear howling all around her.

Thunder clashed, almost deafening in its intensity.

Beth thought she vaguely recognised the place, that it might have been somewhere from her childhood, perhaps the wood that led on from the orchard she and Kathy had played in. But it shouldn't be here, not now. Fearing that her sanity had snapped, she turned around. The cubicles, which she'd hoped to see, weren't there – just the pool and the trees being buffeted by the wind.

"Oh my God," she said and reached for the sink, to try and give herself something solid to hang on to, to try and convince her that what she was looking at wasn't really there.

Her hands clasped empty space and she glanced around, convinced the sink unit would be gone too, leaving her in the middle of nowhere.

She was wrong, the sinks were there. She reached for them and looked into the mirror. Her haunted face stared back, the storm clouds moving quickly, the trees being punished all the more.

"Beth."

At the sound of her name, she whirled around to face the pool, convinced that someone would be standing close by, but the clearing was still deserted. Perhaps she'd heard an animal or a crackle of lighting and her panic stricken mind had made the noise become her name.

"I'm coming for you, Beth."

There was no mistaking that and she looked around frantically, pressing herself against the sink. More thunder crashed overhead and she flinched as the clouds heaved.

Something caught Beth's eye, in the middle of the wind-whipped pond. At first she thought it was a small pile of leaves and twigs, but it seemed to be moving towards the water's edge, as if it wasn't as much at the mercy of the elements as it should have been.

The pile moved closer, rising and strands smoothed out and drooped down, to cover a forehead and temples.

Beth stared open mouthed, her heart pounding, her shoulders rigid with fright. It wasn't a bundle of leaves, it was a person, coming out of the pool in the middle of this storm. She couldn't move or make a sound – not that it would have held any weight over the storm – as the head, shoulders and chest of the person came clear of the water.

It was a woman, her hair plastered to her head, water running down her bare chest. She had no eyes, just dark sockets that ran with dirty water.

"I want you, Beth," said the woman, reaching out with her right hand, leaves and silt covering her fingers. Her voice was steady and Beth could hear her clearly.

125

"What do you mean?" yelled Beth, the wing rising and snatching away her words.

The woman tilted her head and smiled. A stray hair, caught in the wind, slashed against the socket of her left eye. Beth put her hand to her mouth, trying to swallow back the sudden rush of nausea.

"You have something for me, Beth, something that's inside of you."

It took a moment for her to work it out. "My baby?" she screamed. Was that what this was? A waking nightmare, concern about her baby and her future all wrapped up into one awful vision?

The woman stepped out of the water, the leaves and mud depressing around her feet. Even though her eyes were gone, Beth could feel the woman's gaze on her, sizing her up. Instinctively, she put her hands to her belly.

"Why hide what you know I can already see?"

"Leave me alone," screamed Beth, a gust of wind blowing into her face and making her gasp. She turned to the sink, to catch her breath, her fingernails scratching against the porcelain of the basin. "Why are you doing this to me?"

"As soon as I have what I want, Beth, you'll be free of me."

"Who are you?" Beth asked, looking into the mirror as the woman came towards her.

The woman smiled, holding out her arms. "My name is Isabel Mundy, I have come for what is mine."

"But I don't know you." Beth closed her eyes tightly and dug her nails into the palms of her hands, the pain springing tears to her eyes.

"It won't take long," said Isabel, her voice as soft as a lullaby. "It won't hurt you as much as it hurt me."

Beth looked in the mirror. Everything was darker. The clouds were the colour of charcoal, the lightning flashes more frequent now, as if building to an almighty explosion. Isabel came towards her, either not feeling or not caring as her naked body was lashed by the wind and rain.

Beth couldn't work it out, how she could be facing a different world with this woman coming towards her and then felt a surge of anger. She couldn't give in to this, not now. She was carrying a new life, it was her responsibility – what kind of mother would she be to crumble in tears now?

"Trust me," said Isabel. A few more paces and her outstretched hand would touch Beth's shoulder.

That wasn't going to happen. "No," she screamed, as loudly as she could, "don't you fucking touch me."

Her defiance struck Isabel and Beth noticed the slightest frown and faltering of pace. But the frown cleared and she moved forward again.

"It's only fair, Beth."

"You're not having my baby, you fucking psycho."

Isabel stopped and tilted her head as a flash of lightning broke from the clouds and struck a tree behind her, sending a shower of sparks into the pool. She reached out, her fingers long and thin and white. "This won't take long."

"No," screamed Beth, "leave me alone."

Isabel's reflection shimmered slightly. "Don't fight me, it'll just make it worse for you."

"I don't care."

Isabel's reflection shimmered again and the part of the sky that was visible above the trees faded to black, the clouds fraying at their edges and bleeding into it.

Beth crouched down to avoid Isabel's grasping fingers and screamed, "No!". As she did, the clouds lost all semblance of shape and form in the black sheet above the trees. Isabel howled in agony and then she too was gone.

Beth felt tears running freely down her cheeks. The sound of the storm died quickly, until all she could hear were her own sobs.

Slowly, she stood up and looked in the mirror, her haunted reflection staring at her. Behind her were five cubicles, the gleaming tiled walls and the portraits of the Hollywood Greats.

Beth breathed deeply and wiped her hands over her face – her skin was clammy and cold.

The door shushed and she turned quickly, expecting the worst but saw a woman in shorts and a T-shirt come in, her flip-flops squelching on the tiles.

"Bloody hell," said the woman, "are you alright?"

Beth turned to the sink, ran the cold tap and patted the water on her face. "I think so," she said.

"You don't look it, love," said the woman and went into the first cubicle.

Beth looked at herself in the mirror.

"Fucking hell," she said quietly and went over to the towel to dry her face.

CHAPTER 14

BETH STOOD AT THE banister, looking out of the picture windows at the sky, which was dappled with the golden colours of twilight.

Out here, in the real and rational world where hallucinations had no place in the scheme of things, she felt safer. Seeing Isabel Mundy had scared her in a way she couldn't express and she was fretful of her mental state. Could it have been her thought processes working themselves out over everything in such a way that she saw the results physically? Or something much, much worse?

She thought about what Rosie had said to her, a cloud of negative energy gathering over Heyton with the disappearance of Toby. They hadn't found him yet, as far as she knew, so could that bad energy stew, like a neglected cup of tea? If she'd come here feeling down anyway, that kind of atmosphere would just make everything worse.

The toilet door creaked and Beth's shoulders stiffened. She waited for the slap of bare feet, but instead heard the squelch of flip-flops.

"How are you, love?" asked the woman, close enough that they could talk quietly but not so close that she would seem intrusive.

"I'm fine, really, I just had a funny turn, that's all."

"So it seemed. Are you sure you're okay?"

"I'm fine, honestly," said Beth, touched at the woman's concern.

"Good." The woman patted her shoulder and then squelched her way down the stairs.

Beth rubbed her face, took a deep breath and followed the woman downstairs.

Behind the curtains, the auditorium door was closed and she opened it slowly. Maurice was sitting on a fold-down seat, watching the film with rapt attention and he didn't turn around as she closed the door gently. She made her way up the stairs as best she could in the poor light and found their row.

Rob glanced up as she sat down. "Hey, I was getting worried about you. Are you okay?"

"Yes," she said quickly, having made the decision that she wouldn't tell Rob what had happened. If she did, it might open the whole can of worms and she didn't think he was ready for it – she knew she wasn't. And what if she told him the story and he thought she was as mad as she herself did?

"You were gone a while."

"Uh huh," she said and gestured vaguely gesture towards her belly, hoping he would accept that as an answer.

He watched her hand, then looked her in the eyes. "Are you in pain? We can go if you want, if that'd help?"

"No." She smiled and leaned over, kissing him gently on the lips. "Everything's fine now."

"Sure?"

She wasn't, but she felt more secure being next to him in the darkness, feeling his warmth and closeness.

"Yes," she said and snuggled into his side, "let's watch the film."

~

Steve drove back into Heyton, pissed off, his mood not helped by the woman from The Happy Cow screaming and shouting at him from the boot.

He hadn't seen anyone else to take – everyone seemed to be with another person and Steve didn't know how he would deal with that, he certainly wasn't ready to contemplate murder. His desire to serve Isabel was clouding his mind to most things, but he was aware enough to realise that the less attention he drew to himself, the easier he could fulfil his task and the quicker he would be with Isabel forever. Kidnapping a pregnant woman from a group or her attentive partner would surely bring the police down on his head and then what could he do, locked away?

It was getting late, the sky barely lit by faint embers of light as he drove through the docks, looking around in desperation. If he saw a prostitute with a glow, he might snatch her – her disappearance might not be noted for a while.

But he didn't see anyone and wondered if Isabel would be angry with him.

He pulled onto Marine Road, the crowd of revellers greater now than it had been. Within their midst, he could see the glow around certain women even clearer in the poorer light, which just made his sense of frustration and failure worse.

Perhaps he could explain this to Isabel. Surely there had to be some point where Isabel would accept that he'd done his best in only bringing her only one woman without drawing attention to both her and what he was trying to do.

He waited at the traffic lights as a hen party crossed the road, trying not to see which of them had glowing bellies and failing miserably.

"Fuck," he said and, as soon as the lights were on green, he accelerated away, making a few of the stragglers hurry their pace.

The Fair was packed and he groaned. The road alongside it was jam packed with cars and people were milling along the pavement, or queuing up at the burger vans that had pitched for business. The rides, when they cleared the fence, were packed, with every seat taken. Coloured lights rippled across the site and the air was filled with laughter, screams and the churning of heavy machinery.

Now what? Driving around aimlessly would just make him feel worse, but he couldn't park up in case someone heard the woman in the boot and reported it.

He drove past the Fair and The Yard and parked in front of the warehouse. He got out, locked the car and stood quietly for a moment. The woman in the boot yelled something, but the sound was muffled and blended in nicely with the screams and shouts from The Fair.

He walked over to The Yard and went in, sitting on the bench across from the memorial. He thought about last night, when he'd watched Isabel take the baby from Mandy and it made him feel a bit better, that he and Isabel had something between them.

There was also a contradictory feeling, hidden somewhere deep in his mind, that felt nauseous about what Isabel had done. He couldn't put his finger on it, but kept seeing flashes of a small boy, running in a park and laughing loudly.

He shook his head, not wanting to think like that. All he wanted to do was serve Isabel – any other thoughts might detract from that, which he didn't want to have happen.

He looked around, his eyes more accustomed to the gloom and checked he was alone.

"Hello Isabel," he said quietly, "I have another woman for you."

The shouts and screams from the fair sounded loud to him. He leaned forward, his hands linked between his knees.

And she glows?

He sat up, happy and startled at the same time. "Yes, she does. I could only get one though, I didn't want to take any risks."

That was wise. Tomorrow, there is a specific one that I want you to get for me. I have been aware of her for a while, but tonight we saw one another clearly. She is a danger to me, my familiar, and I must have her.

"Couldn't I get her now?"

She is not alone, it would be too dangerous. Tonight, I will suffice with the woman you have brought me. Where is she?

"In the boot of my car."

Bring her to me.

"But there are a lot of people in the Fair. If I get her now, she'll scream the place down and someone will hear her."

Are you questioning my judgement?

"No," he said quickly, "not at all. But the Fair will close in a while and then I can get her, when nobody is around to hear her."

Then we will wait. You have done well, my familiar.

"Thank you, Isabel, thank you very much."

Now rest. Close your eyes and I will show you the woman that you will bring me.

Steve did as he was told and he felt her touch on his cheeks, moving his head gently. In the darkness, he saw a woman standing in front of a mirror, washing her hands.

She is the one that I want, my familiar.

"Yes, Isabel, as you wish."

～

The film finished a little after ten and, as the lights came up, Beth straightened in her chair and yawned.

"Are you tired?"

She shook her head. "No, just comfortable, snuggled up next to my warm boyfriend in the dark."

Rob smiled and stroked her cheek. "Good, I thought the film had sent you to sleep."

"No, it was good," she said and meant it. It was slower than she'd remembered it being, but it had held her attention and Grace Kelly had looked lovelier than ever. "Did you enjoy it?"

He kissed her. "Uh huh. Thank you for this, Beth, it's been the perfect end to a perfect day."

She nodded, glad now that she hadn't told him about her hallucination.

They joined the line of people making their way down the stairs, where Maurice held the door open, wishing each customer a good evening as they passed him.

It was dark now and the picture windows reflected back their shimmering, ghost-like images, pierced occasionally by points of light from the pier and road. Rob took her hand and they went out into the warm night.

"That was excellent," he said and held her close to him.

She hugged him back, her face buried in his neck. She didn't want to let him go.

"Do you want to grab a bite to eat or get something to drink?" he asked and she shook her head as best she could. "Slow walk back to the hotel then?"

She raised her head. "Yes, let's take in the night air."

"And avoid the drunks?" he said and laughed.

"Something like that."

He let go of her and Beth felt a slight pang of panic until he took her hand. Feeling his fingers wrapped around hers made her feel better and they walked along Marine Road. The pubs and arcades were still doing good business, as was the Fair, with people milling around at the entrance and by the burger vans.

A family walked past them, the father pushing a buggy with two sleeping children in it, the mother with her arm hooked through his, her head against his shoulder. Both of them looked happy but tired.

As they passed, the father nodded at Rob and the mother said, "Goodnight folks." She sounded like she was on the verge of laughter.

Beth wondered why she couldn't feel like that, happy and always laughing, back to feeling how she had yesterday when they'd arrived, the coming weekend an unexplored territory in front of them, away from home and its problems.

He stopped and pulled her to him. "Tell me what's wrong."

She chewed her lip, torn between doing as he asked and protecting him from what she was going through. He hadn't even wanted to come here, but now he was enjoying it and all she wanted was to head back to London and get on with things in a place where she didn't see ghosts in dining rooms and didn't have hallucinations in public toilets. How would he react to that?

"I just don't feel right," she said eventually. Now wasn't the time or place.

"Is it the baby?" he asked, the concern clear in his voice.

"No, I don't think so. I just feel…" She let the sentence drift away, scared that everything might slip out if she said another word.

"Tired? Poorly? Is this something to do with why you were so long in the toilet?"

"I'm tired," she said quickly, "that's all. It must be the sea air, the sunbathing this afternoon."

"Or being snuggled up to me in the cinema."

She forced out a brief laugh. "Something like that. Come on, Mr Warren, take me home."

He kissed her forehead and squeezed her hand. "Your wish and all that," he said, smiling.

~

Beth lay in the darkness, Rob beside her asleep, his warm hand on her belly.

She stared at the thin slice of light across the ceiling, thinking.

As she'd showered, trying to wash the day from her body, she'd tried to figure out what to do next and was convinced that her sanity depended on getting out of Heyton. She didn't know how the town could have any kind of influence over her, but the incidences and episodes she was having were getting more intense and she knew she couldn't go through something like the cinema toilet again – it had taken enough courage just to look in the bathroom mirror here. But Rob would want to know why she felt the need to cut their long weekend short.

That was her dilemma. He was enjoying himself and he deserved to know the truth. Even if he didn't believe her, he would have to see that she believed.

Beth closed her eyes, willing sleep to come. She'd think of something.

~

At midnight, Steve decided it was time to get the woman from his car. The Fair had closed and nobody had come past The Yard for a long time. The pubs and clubs on the strip would still be packed, but the patrons would head away from him, back to their houses or B&Bs.

He got to the car and checked to make sure that nobody was around. Satisfied, he slid the key into the lock gently and grimaced as it clicked open. The woman didn't make any noise and he hoped she was asleep.

He put his keys in his pocket and pulled the boot open. When it was at its height, the woman launched herself at him, her head catching him in the belly and winding him.

Steve fell back, clutching his belly, gasping. The woman's forward momentum carried her out of the boot and she fell on top of him, her elbow catching the pavement and making her cry out. He pushed her off and rolled to one side, trying to grab her as she got to her feet.

His fingers snagged the hem of her long skirt and he held it fast. She ran towards the bright lights of the strip, the slack in her skirt playing out for a moment before he felt his arm jerk. He didn't let go and she went over, crying out in pain again.

Keeping hold of her skirt, Steve got to his knees, feeling sick now but able to take deeper breaths. The woman was on all fours, crying.

"Get up," he hissed, grabbing a handful of her hair and climbing unsteadily to his feet.

The woman didn't move so he tugged hard on her hair. "Get up, you stupid bitch."

The woman, all fight gone now, stood up, her legs unsteady.

"It didn't have to be like this," he said and dragged her towards The Yard.

The woman was sobbing, but he kept hold of her hair, waiting for her to make another break for freedom.

"Just do whatever you've got to do," she said. "I don't suppose you'd care, but I'm pregnant."

"I know, that's why you're here. But I've already told you, you're going to be okay."

"What?"

"I have someone I want you to meet."

At that, she did try to pull away and he felt some of her hair come away in his fingers. She cried out and put her hands over his.

He pulled her into The Yard and the woman, as much as she could against his tight grip, looked around as if expecting to see other people waiting for her.

"Please don't rape me, okay? I'll do whatever you want, anything at all, just don't hurt my baby."

Steve stopped in front of the memorial and forced her onto her knees.

"Is that it? Do you want a blow job?"

He laughed. "No, I want you lie down."

"Please," she said and sobbed, "don't rape me. My baby…"

He let go of her hair and slapped her face and she fell back. He knelt on her thighs, pulling her skirt down and her top up, exposing her belly from her panty line to the bottom of her bra.

Move away now, my familiar.

Steve glanced around. Isabel was standing in front of the memorial and he so wanted to go to her, but she held up her hands.

Let me see her.

"Yes," he said, "of course."

He got off the woman, never taking his eyes from Isabel.

The woman turned her head in the grass, watching him go. "What are you doing?" she sobbed.

Ignoring her, he backed away until his shoulder hit the bench. He pulled himself up onto it, unable to take his eyes off of Isabel as she walked gracefully towards the woman.

Now, my pretty.

The woman snapped her gaze towards the memorial, seeing Isabel for the first time. She let out an almighty scream and Steve looked around quickly, sure that somebody would have heard it.

Isabel knelt and put her hands on the woman's belly, chanting. The woman's face screwed up in pain, her hands clawing uselessly at Isabel's and she screamed again and again.

Steve closed his eyes and when the sound of a baby squalling filled the air, he shivered.

He didn't know how long it had been before Isabel touched his chin gently. He opened his eyes, staring into hers.

It's done. Take the woman.

"Have I served you well?"

You have, my familiar, and soon, we will be together. Tomorrow, bring me the woman I showed to you.

"I will, I promise."

Isabel gently stroked his groin and kissed him, then walked back to the memorial, losing definition in the darkness as she did so.

Steve stood up, his erection feeling good. The woman was on her side now, sobbing and he went over and scooped her up in his arms.

"You fucker," she said, looking at him with unfocussed eyes, "you said I wouldn't be hurt."

"It could have been worse," he said and laughed.

Beth knew she was dreaming when she looked down at herself and saw the loose dress of rough fabric.

It was two months since Isabel had met Charity Astor, when John did to her what she'd wished he would do since she'd first met him.

Charity's pregnancy was hard and she found it difficult most days to get out of bed. Isabel went out to the fields every day with John, hoping each time that he would kiss her.

The day he did, it was hot – the sun high and the heat heavy, both of them sweating with exertion.

"We should eat in the wood," John had said, "out of the heat."

She followed him into the trees that marked the edge of his land and, in the shade, she felt better. She drank from the flagon of water that John carried on his belt and he peeled off his shirt. Isabel tried not to stare at his chest.

"Do you like me?"

"I do not know what you mean," she said, embarrassed.

"I can see your nipples," he said and laughed, not unkindly. "I am a married man and I know what it means when nipples get hard and there is no wind." He cupped her chin. "Have you ever been with a man?"

Shocked, Isabel looked at the ground. She wanted, more than anything, for John to take her but didn't want it at the same time.

"I can show you, if you would like." He pressed her face into his sweaty chest and she licked his salty nipple.

"You learn well," he said and pushed her onto her back, stripping her quickly. He kissed her roughly and penetrated her. It hurt like nothing she'd ever felt before, but got slowly better.

Afterwards, he held her closely.

"You must mention this to no-one," he said.

"Of course."

"We can do it again, but you must never act to me like that if Charity is here."

"I will not, I promise."

~

Their assignations continued, mostly in the wood and she began to use her powers to help them in their work. She was sure that he knew she was doing it, but he didn't say a word, seemingly happy to see the crops tended to, allowing him more time in the trees with her.

One Friday morning, Charity had complained of stomach pains like she'd felt with the other births, but she shooed John and Isabel out, telling them she'd be fine.

Isabel had made sure that most of the work in the field was done before they got there and John led her into the wood, walking along dense trails until they finally came to a pond.

Isabel pulled off her dress and dove into the murky water. John followed her and they splashed one another for a while, before kissing. He carried her to the bank and made love to her.

After, they laid in each other's arms and looked up at the clear blue sky, visible through the branches.

She knew she must tell him her news now, or keep her peace forever. "I love you, John."

"You must not say that, Isabel," he said, sternly.

"But it is the truth. As the mother of your child, I must love you."

She felt his body tense. "Mother of my child? No, that cannot be."

"Do you not love me?" There was a silence and she looked into his eyes. "You put this child into me, my love."

He glared at her. "You have bewitched me, Isabel Mundy."

Startled, she sat up and put her arm across her breasts. "What do you mean?"

"Bewitched me, as you have the fields. I can think of nothing but you and these feelings are all your wicked doing."

"Don't say that," she said, tears welling in her eyes. Yes, she'd used her powers to give them time for their love making, but she'd never used them on him, even though she'd wanted to. The way he felt wasn't her fault.

"It must be true. Charity is heavy with child and I lie here with you, a slut who has made me forget what is important."

Isabel began to cry. "But you know that is not true."

"It is, for you are with child. That cannot happen, it must not happen." He got up and pulled his clothes on quickly. "I must get home. You will pack your things and go."

She grabbed his leg and pulled it tight to her. "Please, John, do not make me go."

He kicked her away. "You little witch whore," he yelled. "Charity is my wife. She has treated you with kindness and respect and this is how you repay her?"

"No, John," she sobbed.

He scowled and stalked away through the trees. Isabel quickly dressed and chased after him but he had a good lead and, as she got in sight of the cottage, he was already at the front door.

It had barely closed when she heard his roar of anger and pain. The chilling sound stopped her.

The front door burst open and John screamed at the sky, holding a pink bundle in his arms.

"Isabel Mundy," he yelled, seeing her, "you are a witch and I condemn you to death."

He gently put the bundle down and ran at her.

Isabel, fearing for her life, turned and ran.

~

Beth jolted awake and looked around quickly to make sure that it had been a dream, that she was still in bed in the Clairmont.

Rob moaned in his sleep and turned over, his hand slipping off her belly.

Beth looked at the clock – it was a little after three. Relieved, she looked out of the gap in the curtains at the dark night sky.

It was obvious to her now that the woman in her hallucination was the same as the one she was dreaming of – for some reason, she seemed to be uncovering more about Isabel Mundy. But what was their connection, apart from being with child? She was well aware that dreams shaped themselves from everyday images, twisting them into unreal and surreal sequences, but why see so much? What if what she'd been dreaming about had been some kind of premonition – an episode that had yet to happen, of Isabel coming at her, demanding her child.

She didn't know or understand but she was suddenly convinced that she had to get out of Heyton as soon as she could.

CHAPTER 15

"WAKE UP, BETH."

She opened her eyes slowly, feeling extremely tired, to see Rob leaning over her.

"Come on, sweetheart, we've overslept. I must have turned the alarm off without realising it. I think we've missed breakfast."

"What time is it?"

"Half ten." He stood up and rubbed the back of his head, making his hair stand on end. "We weren't that late last night, were we?"

Beth sat up and yawned. "We must have been more tired than we thought."

"We'll have to go into town for breakfast," he said. He kissed her and went into the bathroom. "They do all day breakfasts out there, don't they?"

"I should think so," she said and he closed the door.

Beth felt a twinge in her belly and rubbed it idly, her mind circling the same thought over and over.

How was she going to get him to leave?

She got out of bed and walked to the window, pulling the curtains open. There were a lot of people on Marine Road, enjoying their holiday and she could see children playing on the beach under the blazing sun.

Everything outside was as normal as it should be at a seaside resort and looking at it stopped her short. Suddenly, the incident in the cinema seemed a long way away and the dreams felt fragmentary, like they may have been a fictional dream themselves but the uncertainty remained. Not fear, exactly, but she knew what she'd seen and felt over the last couple of days and she couldn't easily explain any of it. But how could she persuade Rob of that? He would try to believe her, like always, but he could also just point out the window at the people having a good time on an English beach.

No, it didn't matter. Even if he did that, even if he effectively laughed at her fears – which she knew, deep down, he wouldn't – then she could still go home herself.

The toilet flushed and the shower started. She sat on the bed.

She would make him believe.

Steve came to gradually, his eyes struggling to cope with the darkness and make out objects and surfaces. He'd been dreaming, the remnants of it escaping him like shards of smoke in the wind.

What he could remember didn't make sense. He was on a beach, the sand warm under his feet. A pretty woman, with a round face and blonde hair, was holding the hand of a small boy in a T-shirt and trunks. They were waving and moving down the beach, away from him.

He didn't recognise them but felt a pang at their leaving that struck him in the chest like a well-placed punch.

Steve shook his head, still not clear as to who they were. But who cared? He couldn't start worrying about things like that.

He'd been lying against a wall and sat up, leaning against it as his eyes adjusted. He was in a plain room, the only light a thin strip under the door. He rubbed his eyes and heard, faintly, someone crying.

It all came back to him. He was in the warehouse. He'd felt drained and tired last night, after locking the woman away and had decided to lie down.

He stood up and shook the cramp out of his arm and legs, but his joints still felt stiff. No matter. He pulled open the door and stepped into the corridor.

The crying was louder out here and he walked to the door he was using as the cell and rested his hand on the handle. It creaked and the crying stopped instantly.

"Help," someone called.

Steve unlocked the door and pushed it open. A strong smell, that reminded him of an abattoir, washed over him, making him gag.

"Oh no," said one of the women, as the other one started to cry again.

When his eyes had adjusted to the gloom he could see Mandy. Somehow she'd managed to snap her bonds and was sitting against the wall, her knees tight to her chest, her wrists still bound.

The other woman was crouched against the wall on the other side of the room, her eyes wide and frantic, tears glistening on her cheeks.

He noticed that neither of their bellies glowed.

"What's your name, love?" Steve asked her.

"Jill," she said. "Please let us go. We won't tell anyone, will we Mandy?" She looked imploringly at her fellow prisoner, who slowly shook her head.

"Don't bother," Mandy said. "He doesn't care about us, he doesn't even bother to give us food."

"Hey," said Steve, "I got you some grub yesterday. Stop whining, alright?"

Mandy sneered at him. "Or what? What do I have to lose? You've kidnapped me, taken my baby, left me to piss on the floor. You're just going to kill me when you've had your fun, so why should I stop whining?"

"He won't kill us," said Jill quickly, "he promised." She looked at Steve. "You won't, will you?"

Steve shook his head. "You're both safe and when the time is right, I'll release you. I'm not going to hurt you and neither will anyone else, I promise."

Mandy laughed sourly. "If you come near me, Todd or whatever your name is, I'll bite your cock off."

Steve laughed and closed the door.

"Don't go," pleaded Jill, "please don't leave us here again."

He locked the door and walked down the corridor towards the loading bay, smiling as Jill screamed for him to come back.

~

By the time Beth finished in the bathroom, Rob was sitting on the bed. He looked up expectantly and smiled at her.

"Any problems this morning?"

She wondered what he meant – he looked happy enough, with just the slightest hint of concern. Had he woken up whilst she was dreaming? "Eh?" she said.

"Being sick, you know?"

She rubbed her belly without thinking about it. "No, thank goodness."

Rob stood up. "Excellent," he said and came to kiss her. "Let's get dressed and we'll go and have some breakfast."

"Yes, boss," she said and saluted him, making him laugh. She put her rucksack on the bed and sorted through the layers of clothes – needless layers now, she thought – and found some underwear.

"I'll go down to reception, see if they've got some pamphlets on things to do around here."

"We could take it easy again, if you want," Beth said, looking up. "I thought you wanted to get a decent sun tan."

"I do, but I don't want us to get bored. Was there anything you wanted to do?"

She didn't look up. Now would be the ideal time to ask him to take her away, to leave the seaside, the sun and the beach and head back to London, but she couldn't do it. "No, let's just go with the flow, shall we?"

"Good idea. I'll meet you down in reception," he said and went out.

"Bollocks," she said and dressed quickly, in shorts and a plain T-shirt.

Why hadn't she told him? She sat on the bed to put on her trainers and reached for her handbag. If she couldn't tell him – and kept seeing normal life and happy families – then it was just going to become impossible and she'd be stuck here, at the mercy of whatever happened.

She took out the photograph, hoping against hope that it would be different now, but it was exactly the same as she remembered it.

She exhaled, looking at the smoke-like woman coming out of the man's back, her long thick hair covering most of her face.

Beth felt a jolt of surprise as her mind made the visual connection. Take away the thick hair in the picture and replace it with sodden hair, plastered to the top of a head. Take away the vicious glint in the eyes and replace them with dark sockets.

"Isabel?" she said slowly. "Fuck." She stuffed the photograph back into the handbag and rushed out of the room and down the stairs, her resolve complete now.

The lobby corridor was deserted and she almost ran along it, not even daring to look in the dining room as she knew Goody June would be in there, enjoying her tea. She'd hoped to bump into Rosie, to try and make some sense out of her cryptic warnings, but didn't see the old woman. Rosie had talked of the negative energy, but that photograph had been taken on their first night here. Was the energy focussing on her? It didn't make sense, but then nothing about what she'd experienced this weekend made the slightest bit of sense.

Rob was sitting in one of the easy chairs in reception, flicking through a small colourful pamphlet. Several more were spread across his lap and he looked up as she came towards him. She slowed her pace so as not to concern him.

"Find anything good?"

He gathered the pamphlets together and stood up. "I think so. We can look at them over breakfast."

She slid her arm through his. "Great idea, because I'm starving."

"That's because you're eating for two," he said.

"Ain't that a fact?" she said and they walked out into the sunshine.

～

The sun felt good so Steve went to sit in The Yard, on the bench across from the memorial.

There were a few families around and all of them gave him a wide berth, some even packing up and moving down to the beach when they saw him. He watched them go, not comprehending why at first and then he looked at himself.

His shirt was dirty and speckled with blood and there was a horrible brown smear across his chest. He leaned his head down, inhaled and groaned. He stank – of sweat and onions and something else, a meaty kind of smell. He was a state. But if Isabel didn't care, then who gave a shit?

Steve tilted his head towards the sun but, after a while, decided that Isabel wouldn't come to him with so many people around so he walked to his car.

When he opened the door, a wave of heat rushed out at him but he got in, feeling the sweat quickly gather on his back and wound the window down. He switched on the radio but the inane chatter of Kit Richards made him switch it straight back off.

Hello, Steve.

He swung around in his seat so sharply he felt the muscles tug in his sides. At the same time, he felt a pang in his chest similar to the one that the remnants of his dream had given him.

Isabel was in the passenger seat, her feet on the dashboard tray, her hair draped over her shoulders and chest. She looked at him, her eyes wide, her lips moist.

With her so close, he felt intoxicated. "Hello," he managed to say.

Don't forget that you must get that woman I showed you.

"I won't, I'll get her now."

She gently took his hand and placed it over her right breast, her nipple hard in his palm. *How does that feel?*

"It feels wonderful, Isabel. I will serve you well."

You will. She moved his hand, massaging her breast. *She has a partner, who is with her now. You will need to deal with him.*

"I will."

She moved his hand down her body until it was between her legs. His fingers slid into her soft folds and he began to stroke, moving them inside her.

Go, my familiar, serve me well and then we can be together.

"Yes," he said and she was gone. Disappointed, he closed his eyes and put his fingers to his nose, inhaling her musky scent as he pictured her moving under his touch. He smiled and licked his fingers.

~

Waiting for Rob, Beth stood on the pavement looking towards the cinema. In daylight, it was just a wonderfully old, gothic style picture palace but she knew she'd never be able to set foot in it again.

She turned to look into Ali's Pantry, which was set into the Cumbria Hotel. They'd eaten breakfast here, in a table next to the wall that separated the hotel from the pavement. She leaned against the wall and folded her arms. Three buildings along were a brace of arcades, Slot-Time the furthest away. She felt her arms prickle with gooseflesh and decided they'd cross the road here, rather than walk past the place.

"Hey, gorgeous, looking for something to do?"

She glanced around as Rob came out of the hotel. He was grinning and she realised that all of his niggles about not getting the Barbados trip were gone now.

Which wasn't going to make her request any the easier to make.

"Shall we nip down to the beach?" she said. "There's something I need to ask you."

He frowned. "Nothing serious, I hope?"

"No," she said and forced out a laugh. "I just want a bit of peace, you know?"

He glanced left to right, taking in the people and the cars and nodded. "Fits in nicely with my plans, actually. There's something I want to say to you as well."

"Nothing serious, I hope?"

He smiled broadly at her. "Nah, not really."

Holding hands, they crossed the road and waited at the central reservation whilst a horse-drawn cart rattled noisily past them.

Across the other lane of Marine Road, in front of the municipal pool, a queue of people had gathered. Some were already wearing swimming costumes and holding towels, whilst others carried holdalls or plastic bags. A child, ice cream smeared around his mouth, was doing his best to evade his mother, who was pursuing him with a handkerchief and laughing.

Once the cart was gone, they crossed the road and skirted the knot of people. Beth wasn't really looking where she was going and when Rob tugged her hand, she glanced up quickly and tried to move sideways, but the gypsy had already seen her.

The woman was walking with purpose, a wicker basket over her right wrist, a handful of heather in her right hand. Beth groaned and tried to look through her, but knew it wouldn't work. It didn't matter where they went – anywhere in the country, but especially in the West End – if there was a gypsy selling heather, they wilfully ignored Rob and went straight for her.

"'Ello there, luvvy," said the woman, her bleached hair catching in a slight breeze and revealing her left ear, which seemed to have at least ten piercings in it. "Lucky heather, only a quid."

"Sorry," said Beth quickly, "I'm not interested."

The woman kept her course, angling herself so that Rob would have to let go of Beth or he'd knock her over.

"Bad luck if you don't take it, my love," said the gypsy, her cheerful expression fading with each step.

"No," said Beth firmly, "I'm really not interested."

The gypsy reached out her hand. Beth tried to move out of the way but wasn't quick enough and the gypsy's cold, rough fingers brushed the back of her hand.

"Hey," said Rob.

The gypsy pulled away like she'd been burnt, her expression changing from annoyance to surprise. She stepped back, her mouth opening and closing, but no sound came.

Beth stared at the woman. "What's wrong?"

The gypsy looked at her and let out a whimper. "You have to go, there's nothing for you here."

"Hey," said Beth and reached for the woman, who flinched away, "what do you mean?"

"Go," said the gypsy and she turned and walked away. Within a few paces, she began to run and was quickly lost in the mass of people.

"Bloody hell," said Rob, "what was that all about?"

Beth looked at her hand, where the gypsy had touched her and rubbed the spot against her shorts. "I don't know," she said finally.

Rob shrugged. "Are you okay? She didn't hurt you or anything?"

"No," said Beth, shaking her head, her insides churning at the thought that the woman could see.

~

Steve leaned against the wall of the crazy golf course that bordered the pathway over the beach and watched as the couple walked towards him, down by the side of the pool.

He'd been watching them since they came out of the Cumbria and, if he hadn't recognised the woman from the images that Isabel had shown her, her glowing belly would have done the trick. He'd waited for the perfect moment and, when it looked as if they were heading towards the beach, he decided to make his move then. There were too many people on Marine Road and he wasn't about to make a mistake now.

As they got closer, he stepped behind a windmill, though he knew that neither of them would recognise him.

~

Beth stood at the top of the steps and looked around.

"What's wrong?"

She rubbed the back of her neck. "Nothing."

Rob put an arm over her shoulders. "You sure?"

"Yes, it's just that I could have sworn…" She looked at the wall and could just see the top of a windmill on the crazy golf course. "That someone was watching us." She shook her head. "It's just me being stupid. That heather seller must have spooked me or something."

"She spooked me, taking off like that."

Beth took his hand. "Come on, I want to hear your news."

～

Steve counted to ten and looked over the wall. They were on the beach now, heading away from him, towards the Fair.

Someone grabbed his arm and he spun around. It took a moment or two to place the frantic face and, when he did, it felt like he hadn't seen the man for years.

"Have you seen Mandy?"

"No," Steve said, pulling his arm out of Chris Valentine's grasp. "Why, should I have?"

"No, I just wondered if you had. She went on a hen night on Friday and she hasn't been home since. I rang the police yesterday but it's too soon, they can't do fuck all. I've rung everybody else that I can think of and nobody's seen her." He shrugged. "I didn't know what else to do, so I thought I'd walk around and see if I could see her." He reached for Steve's arm again. "Are you sure you haven't seen her?"

"Certain," said Steve. "I'd love to help you search but I've got to go."

Chris nodded. "If you see her, you'll let me know, won't you?"

"She'll turn up, Chris, you know she will."

Yes," Chris said slowly. He looked at Steve, as if for the first time. "Christ, mate, you look like shit."

"Thanks, I'll see you later," said Steve and he walked over to the pathway.

"Ring me if you see her," Chris called.

"Of course," said Steve and then Chris was out of sight.

～

149

Beth looked at the fair and stopped. She didn't feel like going into the park today.

"Will here do?" Rob asked.

She glanced around. There were plenty of people on the beach but, like yesterday, most of them were by the pier. "Seems okay," she said and sat on the warm sand.

Rob sat next to her. "Did you want to go first?"

Beth drew her knees up, rested her arms over them and wondered where to start.

~

Steve walked along the path, close to the wall. He thought, for one glorious moment, that they were going to walk by The Yard, but they stopped in front of the Fair.

His foot caught something and he looked down. The lump of brick hadn't come out of the wall, so he didn't know how it had got there, but it seemed like a golden opportunity. He picked it up and measured its weight.

~

"You go first," said Beth.

"Okay," said Rob and he reached into his right pocket.

Beth frowned, shielding her eyes from the sun. "What are you up to?"

He knelt down, his hand closed over whatever had come out of his pocket. "This," he said. "I wanted you to know how I felt, how much I love you and how much I'm looking forward to the baby and us bringing it up together."

Beth felt tears spring to her eyes. "Oh, Rob."

He opened the box and held it out to her. "Beth, I love you so much. Would you…"

Rob didn't get a chance to say anything else. Beth hadn't seen the man coming and it wasn't until he roared with anger that she even knew he was there.

It all seemed to happen in slow motion. The man hit Rob with something, making him cry out and fall sideways, the ring box flying out of his hand.

The man's momentum pushed him into the sand, kicking up a pile of it. He spluttered and rolled over and was on his feet before Beth had a chance to do little more than take a breath.

He came at her like a rugby player and pushed her back into the sand, clamping his right hand over her mouth and nose.

"Don't say a word," he said, "and everything'll be fine. Nod if you understand me."

Beth tried her best to nod, the smell of the man bringing fresh tears to her eyes. She tried to see how Rob was, but the man had her pinned down too well.

"Good," said the man and, keeping his hand over her mouth, dragged her to her feet.

CHAPTER 16

Rob came to, aware of something warm and gritty against his face.

His stomach heaved and he turned his head and vomited.

Groaning, he opened his eyes, shielding them against the glare of the sun with a heavy arm. He sat up as carefully as he could, but still the movement made his head pound and he swallowed back bile, his eyes watering.

He looked over at the roller coaster, trying to remember what had happened. He'd been on the beach with Beth, wondering what she wanted to say to him and he remembered taking out the ring and going down on one knee.

Rob felt something trickle out of his hairline and gingerly touched the spot. Blood dripped off his fingers into the sand.

"Shit," he said and dabbed his temple with his handkerchief, wincing when the material touched the cut.

Cars began to clank nosily up the incline of the roller coaster and the sound brought everything back to him. The angry roar of the man and the sudden, blinding pain that followed.

Beth.

He looked around frantically, ignoring the thumping pains in his head and the stars that burst across his line of vision. He couldn't see her and got shakily to his feet.

A couple were going into the park, negotiating the steps carrying a double buggy between them, the children hanging onto the straps grimly.

Beyond them, by the rocks, was a couple who seemed to be struggling against one another. The glare of the sun felt like it was burning through his retinas, but Rob squinted to try and focus on them.

The woman was wearing shorts and a plain T-shirt. The man was wearing dark trousers and a shirt that seemed to be several different colours.

It could be her, Rob thought and shouted "Beth," his voice making his head thud.

The man turned, saw Rob and yanked the woman, who looked around and screamed "Rob!"

Hearing Beth's voice, full of terror, was like a slap in the face and Rob ran, not caring that his body protested, the dry and loose sand making progress difficult, his only concern to reach them before the bastard made off with her.

Beth was trying to fight the man off, clawing and punching at his face. He wrapped his arms around her and jerked her off her feet and she kicked out, her heels bouncing off his shins.

Rob kept moving, ignoring the pain, not wanting to let them get out of sight around the rocks. He thought he was gaining on them and was across from the park when Beth and her kidnapper disappeared from sight.

"Stop," he yelled, knowing it was useless.

He pushed himself, willing his legs to move quicker in the shifting sand. It felt like he was running in treacle and not getting anywhere, like some kind of terrible nightmare where Beth was taken and he was powerless to do anything about it. Images of her, of what she would have said when he asked her to marry him, seemed to dangle in front of him, staying just out of reach.

As he ran by the rocks, the sand got firmer and his strides took him further. He saw the edge of a dilapidated warehouse with a large sign on its side, which the weather and local vandals, with spray cans and pellet guns, had made unreadable.

Rob cleared the rocks and slowed to a halt, his lungs burning. As he tried to get his breath, the pain came flooding back and, for a moment, he thought he was going to collapse. Another wave of nausea washed over him and he bent his head forward, his hands on his knees and tried to take deep breaths, but couldn't. He gave in and vomited, then looked up and around.

The beach ahead was deserted, his only company a few seagulls further away, arguing over a piece of debris half buried in the sand.

"Fuck," he said, trying to control his growing sense of panic. He couldn't have lost them that quickly and he tried to think it through logically. They must have changed direction.

He looked at the warehouse and saw movement in the shadows of the loading bay. Someone was in there, going up some stairs, heading towards a darker patch of shadow.

It could have been anyone, a security guard perhaps, but he didn't think so.

He ran towards the warehouse and, as the shadows lost some of their darkness, he saw the two people on the bay.

~

Steve looked out into the glare of the beach, the heat haze making it hard to see clearly. But he could see enough – the stupid boyfriend was coming after them.

The woman was still struggling, but Isabel had seemed keen to get her so Steve resisted the temptation to punch her unconscious. He'd wanted to, though. She'd kicked the shit out of his shins, and his left cheek was stinging where one of her punches had landed. But he felt good for all that. He was fulfilling his task and Isabel would be pleased with him.

The woman tried to punch him again, so he lifted her up and swung her around to face the beach.

"See?" he said, his lips close to her ears. Her hair smelt nice and he vaguely recognised the perfume of it. "Your boyfriend's coming for you. And when he does, I've got a real surprise for him."

"Rob," the woman screamed before he could stop her.

Steve clamped his hand over her mouth. "Naughty, naughty, I told you about that."

He backed to the door and pushed the handle down with his free hand. The door swung open and he dragged her through it, kicking it shut.

The corridor was cool and gloomy and he shoved the woman away. She staggered for a couple of steps, before going down on her hands and knees.

"What's your name?"

The woman turned her head to face him and he could see tears glistening on her cheeks. "Fuck off."

"That's not nice," he said and she let out a startled yelp when he lunged at her. He pulled her to her feet and threw her against the wall, her head bouncing off the plasterboard with a dull thud. He put his face close to hers and pinched her cheeks, forcing her mouth into a rough square shape. "I won't hurt you so long as you tell me your name."

She stared at him and he could see the terror in his eyes. He felt like he was on top of the world.

"It's Beth."

He let go of her cheeks and she rubbed them, looking at the floor.

"Please don't hurt me," she said quietly, "I'm pregnant."

"I know you are, Beth, but I'm not going to hurt you. You can trust me."

~

Hearing Beth scream his name had given Rob a fresh surge of energy and he was only a few yards from the loading bay when the couple moved into the darker shadows and disappeared again.

He ran under the warehouse canopy and rushed up the steps, his breathing harsh and echoing off the breeze-block wall. Along the dock, there was a door with a glass panel in the middle of it and he stopped beside it, leaning against the wall whilst he tried to figure out what to do.

He wanted to go in and get her, but would that help? The man obviously knew the place and Rob didn't and he wasn't in that great a shape to fend for himself. But if he went to the park and got someone to call the police, the man could take Beth anywhere and Rob would never be able to forgive himself if anything happened to her.

He opened the door and stepped into the dark corridor. Several doorways opened off it and the corridor ended in a set of double doors. The air was thick with the smell of urine and faeces.

Panic surged through him again and he tried to control it – he had to keep going, he had to find her.

There was a dull thud from behind one of the doors and he was instantly alert, the skin pulling tight across his shoulders and up the back of his skull, his panic dispersing as his heart began to pound.

Another thud, followed by a low voice calling softly, "Help."

He figured out where the sound was coming from, the second door to his right. He passed the first door, then pressed himself to the wall and edged along slowly. Every sound he made – his breathing, the brush of his T-shirt against the plasterboard, the gentle squeak of his trainers – seemed to be amplified out of all proportion and he knew that the man must be able to hear him.

He touched the door handle and took a deep breath.

~

Steve listened to the boyfriend making his way noisily up the corridor and stifled a laugh. If you're going to creep up on somebody, he thought, you should at least do it so they couldn't hear you.

He gripped the cool metal of the door handle and decided to give it another few moments before he sprang his surprise.

~

Rob leaned against the door, to see if he could hear anything from inside the room but it was silent now.

He counted to three in his head and stepped into the middle of the corridor, to position himself better, not letting go of the door handle.

A door opened behind him and, startled, Rob turned to see a man coming at him. He tried to move but the man came in low, his shoulder catching Rob's hip, forcing him back against the wall, the plasterboard creaking under the pressure.

Rob slid to the floor and the man stood over him.

"Thought you could creep up on me, eh?" He leaned down and pressed his finger into the cut on Rob's forehead. "Nasty things, bricks, aren't they?"

Rob winced. "What've you done with her?"

"She's safe. Uncle Steve has taken good care of her."

"If you've hurt her…"

Steve folded his arms. "Yeah? What're you going to do?"

Rob pushed himself off the wall and wrapped his arms around Steve's knees, knocking him off balance and backwards. His shoulder hit the plasterboard, denting it and he fell sideways. Rob sat on his chest and dug his fingers into Steve's neck.

Steve's eyes widened, as he began to choke.

"Where is she?" demanded Rob, surprised to be in control but determined not to let the man away. He pressed harder, moving his right palm around to cover Steve's windpipe. "What've you done with her, you bastard?"

"Can't tell," Steve gasped and jabbed his fingertips into Rob's sides.

The pain was incredible and Rob let go of the man's neck. Steve got up, sliding his back up the wall and he shoved Rob away, kicking out.

Rob tried to avoid the kick but it glanced off his back, just above his kidney. He threw up against the skirting board.

"Lovely," said Steve and pulled Rob to his feet by his hair.

Rob didn't know what part of himself to hold first, there was so much pain. Worse than that, though, was the horrible feeling that he'd blown his advantage.

Steve pushed him against the wall and leaned in close. Even over the smell of his own vomit, Rob could smell the man – a horrible, meaty odour like spoiled meat.

"The more trouble you make for me, the more trouble your lovely girlfriend will be in, do you understand?"

"Yes," said Rob.

"Good." Steve twisted Rob's arm behind his back and pushed him into the door he'd tried to open before. "Open it."

His teeth gritted against the pain, Rob opened the door and the smell of a toilet washed over him. He gagged, his eyes watering, making it even harder to see through the dense gloom of the interior.

"Get in, I'll be back for you later..."

The scream took Rob by surprise and he was vaguely aware of people coming towards him and then they were past. He wrenched himself free of Steve as the screams increased in volume and anger. Steve let out a startled cry and there was a thud.

Standing in the darkness of the room, Rob turned around.

Steve was against the wall, the plasterboard broken around his head, dust in his hair. Two women were on top of him, slapping and punching him but, apart from a couple of feeble efforts, he wasn't doing much to fight them off. The blonde woman was on his lap, slapping his face, her nails digging into his cheeks and drawing blood. The other woman, a brunette, was standing to Steve's left and kicking him in the thigh and ribs. She was the one he was weakly trying to push away, but the woman just kicked his hands down and drove her foot into his groin. Both women were still screaming, the noise echoing along the corridor.

"Hey," shouted Rob, "hey!"

The blonde turned, her expression furious, her voice loud and scratchy. "Are you with him?"

Rob held his hands out. "No. He's taken my girlfriend, I followed them into here."

The blonde slapped Steve again, rocking his head into the plasterboard. Both of his eyes were shut and speckles of blood ran across his eyelids. His lips were split and his cheeks looked red raw.

The blonde stood up and pulled the brunette away.

"Jill," she shouted, holding the brunette's face, "Jill? It's over."

"No, Mandy, it's not," Jill yelled and kicked Steve's feet.

"Yes." Mandy shook her. "It is."

Jill glanced at Rob. "Who the fuck are you? Are you with him?"

"No," said Rob quickly. "I just told you. He took my girlfriend."

Jill glared at him. "I don't believe you."

"I don't care what you believe," he said, angrily. "He took my girlfriend and brought her in here, I didn't know you were here. I need you to go and get help."

Mandy looked at him and there was something in her eyes that struck him as paralysingly sad – he didn't think he'd ever seen a look like it before. "Okay."

"Thank you. I'm Rob Warren and my girlfriend's name is Beth Hammond. This bloke here, Steve, just took her straight off the beach."

Mandy frowned. "He told me his name was Todd."

Rob shook his head, frustrated that she didn't just go and do what he wanted. "It doesn't matter what his name is. He took her and she's here somewhere and I don't know where. And he can't tell me now, can he?"

"She can't be far," said Mandy. "He dragged something down the corridor, so she must be in another office or something."

"I'll look," he said and gripped her shoulders. "But you have to go and call the police and an ambulance."

"Too late for an ambulance," Mandy said bitterly, "I've already lost my baby."

It was said so matter-of-factly that Rob thought he hadn't heard properly, but he knew he had. "When?"

"The other night sometime. That fucker took me into The Yard and I don't remember a lot else, except that by the time I was put in here I didn't have my baby any more. Same with Jill."

The full horror of Mandy's words rained down on Rob like a shower of hail. "Beth is pregnant," he said slowly. "Fuck. Look, just go and get help. Please tell me you'll do that."

"I will. I promise." She touched the side of his face gently. "Thank you, Rob, for saving us."

He shook his head briskly. "Just get a move on, alright?"

Between them, they persuaded Jill to leave Steve alone. She kicked him once more in the groin before allowing herself to be led down the corridor.

"We'll send help," called Mandy as she pulled Jill through the door.

"Go," said Rob and he looked at the office doors, trying to decide which to search first, ignoring the images his mind was churning up of Beth, tied up in a dark room, with blood running out from between her legs.

CHAPTER 17

IN THE CORNER, BETH hugged her knees to her chest and looked around the warehouse. The massive open space housed nothing, except a few packing crates near to the front roller doors. Several steel supports, all of them dented and rusting badly, held up a corrugated roof that had seen better days and most of the clear panels set into it as skylights were broken.

The man who'd grabbed her had literally thrown her in here and left. Although she was scared, she was determined not to idly wait for him to come back, so she checked all the doors she could find but they were locked. The packing crates were empty and she couldn't find anything to use as a weapon. But that didn't matter, she'd use her fists and feet if need be, she wouldn't go easily. Each time she closed her eyes, she saw Rob lying on the beach with blood already gathering on his forehead and his final words echoed through her mind, like a haunting melody that she found unbearably nostalgic. He was going to ask her to marry him and then this bastard had taken it all away from her.

Beth looked around again, hoping there was something she'd missed last time.

"Hello."

Beth glanced around sharply and saw a woman at the back of the warehouse, walking towards her. She seemed to have a sheet wrapped around her, but as Beth squinted in the gloom, she could see that it was a dress, made of rough material.

"Thank God," said Beth, getting to her feet. "I've been locked in here by a maniac and he's hurt my boyfriend."

"I know, Beth," said the woman, skirting the pools of light as she came closer.

"How do you know my name?" Beth stared at the woman, trying to discern the features that were draped in shadow.

"I know a lot about you, as you know a lot about me."

"Isabel Mundy?" Beth's world suddenly seemed to shift. Fear washed through her, filling her mind with a clinging, cloying smoke that ran through her veins and tingled in her fingers and toes.

"Yes. We have so much to talk about, but for now, I must leave you a while. My familiar has not been successful."

~

The whispered cry for help came from behind the last door and Rob opened it gently, wary of someone rushing at him. "Hello?"

"Rob? Oh thank God," said the voice, still whispering.

Relief flooded through him and he thought, for the briefest of moments, that he was going to collapse against the doorframe as tears ran down his cheeks. He'd found her – she was safe.

"Are you hurt?" The only light was from the loading bay door and he couldn't see into the room clearly, the darkness seeming to embrace him. There was an earthy, dank smell in the air.

"No," said the woman and stood up at the back of the office.

He could see her clearly, almost as if she had a spotlight trained on her, but he realised that the light was coming from within her – her face and body glowing a green-ish-white in the gloom.

It wasn't Beth. He looked at the naked woman and wondered how many more Steve had kidnapped.

"You do not seem pleased to see me," said the woman, coming towards him.

Rob backed out of the door. He didn't understand what was going on, but knew it wasn't good. "I need to find Beth," he said.

"But I am Beth," implored the woman.

"No," he said firmly, "you're not."

He didn't know who she was, but she didn't act like she'd been kidnapped. What if she was Steve's accomplice? What if this was worse than he'd originally thought?

The light blinked out, the woman's image glowing on his retinas. He tried to close the door but something cold scuffed the side of his face and he was pulled into the room. The door clattered shut, the darkness complete. The air smelled worse now, of dampness and decay, of something spoiled.

"You do not want her," said the woman, sounding as if she was next to him.

"Yes I do," insisted Rob. "If you or Steve has hurt her, I swear to God that I'll…"

The woman was in front of him, suddenly glowing brightly. "What will you do?"

Rob couldn't speak. He couldn't take his eyes off the woman – he'd never seen anyone so beautiful before. Her hair was a striking red, even in the strange light, her breasts were firm and full and her belly was slightly rounded.

She touched his chin with cool, smooth fingers, smiling. "Beth no longer matters. You are mine now and I am yours. You want me, do you not?"

He knew it was wrong, but she was right. "Yes," he said, but saw himself on the beach, in front of a woman he recognised, with a box in his hand. He tried to remember what was in the box but couldn't.

The woman frowned. "Think not of that, but of me. I am offering myself to you." She ran her hands down his front and stroked his groin. "Would you not like that?"

"I would," he said, but something still didn't feel right. There was something about the box and who he was handing it to.

The woman frowned and put her cool fingers to his temples, wiping out the pain that seemed to have been throbbing there for a long time. She kissed and licked his cut.

"You must wait for me, a little trial of patience." She kissed his lips. "Then we can be together."

"Please don't go."

"Worry not, my familiar, I will return."

~

Beth stared at the roof, her mind trying to make sense of what she knew and she kept coming back to the same conclusion.

As much as she couldn't believe it, everything that she'd gone through this past few days – the dreams and weird feelings, the photograph and the

163

hallucination at The Empire – all of it had been real, leading her to his moment and she'd walked right into it and put Rob in harm's way at the same time. So what did she do now? Sit and accept that this was happening, or try to stop it?

"You cannot stop anything," said Isabel, as she walked out of the shadows, her bare feet slapping gently on the concrete. "I will take your child and have my revenge."

"But what have I ever done to you?"

"You know this town robbed me of my child."

"You're insane," said Beth, "how could I know that?"

"Because you can see." There was a loud hissing noise that made Beth flinch and then Isabel was next to her, cool fingers stroking her cheek. "They hunted me down like an animal," she said and pressed her right palm on Beth's forehead.

~

"Kill the witch!"

Isabel risked a glance over her shoulder and saw a dozen men coming for her, some carrying farm equipment that they'd no doubt use if they caught her.

"She's heading for the wood," shouted John Astor and something curdled inside her. How could he do this, after what she'd told him? She didn't deserve this, what happened hadn't been her fault.

She looked ahead, trying to keep up her pace. The wood wasn't far, only a dozen or so yards and, once she was in there, she could hide or keep moving and they wouldn't know which she'd decided to do.

Stones rained around her, kicking up puffs of dirt and one whistled past her head. She ducked and stumbled, but managed to stay upright and then she was in the trees.

The sunlight was suddenly gone and she ran blindly for a few steps, branches reaching for her and snagging her hair and dress. As her eyes grew accustomed to the light, she changed her path, thorns and brambles pricking her bare soles. Each stride took her deeper into the woods, towards the pond. If she could get past that, it might throw them off and give her time to reach the road and perhaps persuade a coachman or farmer to give her passage, to get her far away from Heyton.

She didn't see the thick twist of bramble and it looped around her ankle, pulling tight and bringing her down. She cried, in pain and pity, as she pulled the thick stem and its thorns out of her shin, blood running freely down her ankle and foot and through her fingers.

Holding a tree for support, she stood and tested her leg. The pain was harsh, any pressure causing fresh blood to stain the mulchy earth, but it wasn't broken. She wiped her bloody fingers on her dress and someone crashed into the undergrowth close by.

Startled, she ran but the woods were harder to negotiate than she'd thought they would be. She listened as the men spread out behind her, calling to each other, suggesting different paths.

She came to a fallen tree and recognised it, knew she was almost at the pond. She cut through some nettles, down a small incline, but stumbled and skinned her knees.

Isabel stayed on all fours, trying to catch her breath, her lungs and legs burning, her ankle feeling like it was on fire. She couldn't run much further, but she refused to give up and managed to get to her feet. She staggered down the incline, past another tree.

There was the pond. An hour ago, its water had looked cool and inviting, now it seemed murky and stagnant, full of hidden dangers.

She heard the man a moment before she felt his boot in her back and then she was sprawled on the ground. She looked up at the angry faces, their breathing heavy and laboured in the quiet of the clearing and knew she was dead.

"You are a feisty one," said someone, as out of breath as the others, but sounding more dignified and important.

She looked over and saw Reverend Duncan, his white hair unruly and snagged with leaves, his cassock dirty and ripped in a couple of places. He clasped his hands at his chest. "John Astor, are you sure of what you say?"

"I am," said John and Isabel felt like screaming. "She bewitched me, tricked me into giving her a child and then killed mine own. Charity was crying over the abomination when I returned home and it was already dead, killed by this whore's hand."

"We must test this," said the Reverend, "before we go further."

"Do you doubt me?" demanded John. "How many more must she kill before you believe me?"

"A witch must die for her sins," said someone else.

"We will test her in the pond, Reverend," said John and grabbed her right upper arm. More rough hands grabbed her and she was lifted up and carried to the edge of the water.

"Lord forgive us," intoned the Reverend, "but we must test the child for the evils of witchcraft."

"John Astor seduced me," cried Isabel, "and put his child in me. I did nothing to his child."

"Liar," he yelled and pinched her skin hard enough to draw blood.

They dropped her and she rolled over, staring at the unforgiving, angry eyes. John spat on her when she looked at him.

"Look at the blood all over her," said a man she didn't recognise, "that is the blood of the Astor child."

"Child-killing witch," snarled John, kneeling at her feet. He grabbed her dress and ripped it, the others joining in until Isabel was lying naked.

"Oh Lord," said the Reverend, "the mark of the witch is upon her."

Now all was lost. The line of moles on her belly had been with her for years and her mother had assured her similar could be found on town constables, magistrates or priests, though witchcraft would never be uttered against them; only her.

"Please, John," she said, "you have seen them before. Do not let them do this to me, consider our child."

He looked at her, aghast. Bellowing his rage, he picked her up and threw her into the pond. The water was shockingly cold and she kicked for the surface, though she knew she was going to die because there were too many of them against her, in her hurt and weakened state.

She broke the surface and gulped air, the water stinging her eyes, her hair plastered to her face. She heard splashes and then calloused hands were on her shoulder, pushing her under before she'd taken a full breath.

She reached for her attacker, trying to dig her nails into him, but the water slowed her and, too soon, her lungs craved for air.

Fingers twisted in her hair and pulled her up. She broke the surface, gasping, but was pushed under again before she could fill her lungs and she felt giddy and sick. Water rushed down her throat, choking her.

She was pulled up again and vomited bile and brackish water over the man who'd been holding her down. He pushed her away, disgusted.

"She lives," called the Reverend, standing on the bank, crossing himself. "Duck her again."

With this warning, Isabel took in a lungful of air before she was forced under the water. More hands pressed her down and someone kicked the back of her legs.

She opened her eyes, trying to see in the churning water and vaguely made out the shape of the man holding her down. She reached for him, touching his knee and, once she knew where he was, concentrated hard.

She felt quick, sharp pains in her fingertips as chords of what seemed like rope burst out of them. They snaked through the water and wrapped themselves around the man's groin. She heard his howl of pain clearly, as he let go of her and she was pulled to the surface.

The man was leaning against the bank, screaming in agony, blood colouring the water around him.

Isabel was wrenched around to face John, his face contorted with anger. He slapped her cheek hard, knocking her back into the water. Hands pulled her up and he hit her again.

"John!" called the Reverend, "that is not right."

"She is a witch and a whore, Reverend, it is all she deserves."

She was pulled back up for John to hit her again and again and she felt bones break in her face. Soon, the churning water was tinged scarlet.

"Do you confess?" bellowed John.

The pain was incredible, but still she didn't give up. "I confess that you brought me here, John and had your way with me and now you say that it was I who bewitched you, not the other way around."

John punched her. She fell into the water and saw the men move towards her, their outlines hazy and uneven and she welcomed the shrouds of darkness that cloaked her vision.

When Isabel opened her eyes, she hoped she was dead and that her mother was waiting for her with open arms. But the pain came back in an instant and she knew she was alive.

She could see the sky, darker now, the undersides of the clouds tinged with pink. Around her were damp slabs of stone and she was lying on something cold and rough.

"Isabel Mundy," intoned the Reverend, out of sight, "you have been found guilty of witchcraft and sentenced to death."

"By whom?" she called, the words slurred by her broken jaw.

The Reverend appeared above one of the stone slabs. "You survived the trial by water," he said, "and now you will be buried in stone, to keep your evil spirit away from the good folk of Heyton."

Isabel panicked when she realised that the stone slabs around and under her were her burial chamber. She tried to sit up but every inch of her seemed to scream in pain and she couldn't move.

Part of the sky was blocked, as stone scraped stone and she closed her eyes, willing her aching and weary body to find strength from somewhere, to stop this.

She bit her lip, the pain jagging through her, clearing her mind for the briefest of moments.

In her mind's eye, she could see a man pushing the slab, his heart beating in his chest. She watched her translucent hand reach into his chest, her fingers encircling his pounding organ and slowly squeezing. "Die," she hissed.

There was a gurgle and a dull thud.

"It is her," someone called, "he is dead by that witch's hand."

"Quickly," said another, "get the stone before she finishes us all off."

"Die," she hissed again, her mind's eye searching for John. She found him, her fingers caressing his heart before squeezing it abruptly. She heard him gasp and fall.

She moved her hand into more chests, heard more death, until the sound of the stone scraping stone drowned everything out.

"I curse you all," Isabel screamed. "For taking my life and that of my unborn child, I will one day return and take all of your unborn children."

"Quickly," someone yelled.

"I curse you all," she screamed and the stone slid into place, leaving her in darkness.

~

Rob opened his eyes to darkness, not sure where he was.

He felt around for the woman, but she'd gone and he felt sad and somehow hollow, like he'd done the wrong thing and regretted it.

Images played in his mind again, of him on the beach with a box, but they stayed, frustratingly, just outside of his grasp. Whatever the images meant, he was sure they were responsible for the hollow feeling. Who had he been on the beach with? What was in the box? And how could they interfere with the feeling of elation that he knew he should be enveloped in, with this woman literally throwing herself at him.

He stood up and felt his way to the door.

~

Beth slowly focussed on the opposite side of the warehouse as the last remnants of Isabel's death dispersed into the air, though she could still feel the cold of the slab against her back and buttocks.

"So now you know what they did to me," said Isabel.

It had been a terrifying vision, more so than any of her episodes had ever been. "I'm sorry for what happened to you, but what does your curse have to do with me?"

"Everything," said Isabel quietly.

Beth tried to sound strong, but knew her voice would crack and betray her. "You are not having my child, Isabel."

"Is that how you beg now? Not on your knees, in the posture of prayer, with tears running down your cheeks?"

Beth dropped to her knees and clasped her hand, her tears natural and unforced. "I'll beg if you want, but please, don't do anything to my baby."

"Too late. This town must be shown that they were wrong to do what they did to me."

She stepped towards Beth, who quickly got up and backed away, arms reaching behind her for the support pillars. Tears were spilling from her eyes now, blurring her vision so that she could only make out the vague shape of Isabel, the woman coming to her with outstretched arms.

Beth's right arm brushed a cold surface and she glanced at it. Her attention was only distracted from Isabel for a moment, but it was enough. When she looked up, Isabel wasn't coming for her any more.

"Did you think you could run?"

Beth turned. Isabel was beside her, her mouth fixed into a malicious grin, her eyes wide and staring.

"No," said Beth, trying to get back the rage she'd felt for her kidnapper, but standing up to Isabel now wasn't like it had been at The Empire.

Isabel slapped Beth, knocking her to the floor and knelt by her head.

Close up, the woman was ever so slightly translucent.

"Now we can begin," she said and deftly moved sideways, to sit on Beth's lap, pinning her wrists down easily.

Beth tried to free her hands and Isabel leaned down, her face only inches from her Beth's, her breath like nothing she'd ever smelled before – it was rotten, but not quite; old and musty, but not quite. It was the smell of freshly dug earth, but also the smell of wet stone. It was all of this at once and more. Beth gagged.

Isabel kissed her forehead and moved back, so that she was sitting on Beth's thighs. Beth felt cool fingers at the hem of her T-shirt, moving towards her breasts, rucking the material and then in the waistband of her shorts, pulling them down beyond the line of her panties.

Beth struggled, flailing her arms and trying to rock her body, but Isabel shrugged off the blows.

"You are not strong enough," she said.

Beth felt Isabel's smooth fingertips drawing intricate patterns on her belly.

"Now we begin," intoned Isabel slowly.

At first, the pain was like a nagging itch that couldn't be reached and didn't feel like it was coming from one specific area. Then the pain quickly got worse, until it felt like something was inside her and clawing to get out, wearing razor-tipped gloves.

Beth screamed and tried to roll to one side, to dislodge Isabel, but the woman's knees were on the ground, keeping her well anchored. Gritting her teeth, Beth looked at Isabel's hands and thought, at first, that she must have gone mad.

Isabel's fingertips were inside her. Beth could see her hand, the smooth back of it, the long fingers, all the way to the last knuckle where her own skin was penetrated. She struggled afresh, the pain getting worse all the time and starting to cloud her mind. Bright bursts of light flashed at the edge of her vision and her heart beat a vicious tattoo in her chest. She bit her lip hard enough to draw blood, so that she didn't faint. She had to stay conscious, had to fight Isabel off.

"Give in to me," Isabel shouted at her.

"Fuck off," screamed Beth and spat blood at the woman.

Isabel wiped her face and licked her fingers clean, then moved herself to get a better position.

With the weight off her briefly, Beth tried to drag herself away and, for a moment, she thought she was succeeding. Her elbows gained purchase but more pain hit her, a heavy wave that made her vision darken and she lay back, unable to fight it any more.

~

Rob frowned at the body that was slumped in the corridor. Who was that? He was about to go and see when there was an almighty scream from behind the double doors at the end of the corridor, the voice driving something into his mind like a sharpened spike.

Suddenly, everything was clear and he ran for the double doors.

~

Beth felt herself slipping away, the waves of pain washing through her now almost too much to bear. She still tried to claw Isabel, but she didn't have the energy and closed her eyes, wanting to be taken away from this horror.

Vaguely, she heard a clicking sound and hoped it was somebody, anybody, coming to her aid.

"What's going on?"

Beth felt a surge of hope at Rob's voice that pushed away the barriers of pain for a moment.

Isabel howled with anger and the pain ebbed a little. Beth opened her eyes to see that Isabel was looking past her, an annoyed expression on her face. But it wasn't Isabel's face that drew her attention. It was her hands.

They were six inches above Beth's belly, green-ish tendrils of what seemed to be a mixture of smoke and mucus coming from her fingertips. Beth followed them down, to where they were buried in her belly.

She screamed and managed to roll her body to one side. Isabel, her attention distracted, was knocked off balance and leaned back to steady herself.

It was all Beth needed.

With a surge of energy she didn't realise she had, Beth sat up and put her hands over Isabel's face, pushing backward. Isabel's weight pressed her upper legs to the floor, but Beth ignored the pain.

Finally, Isabel flopped backwards, her head bouncing off the floor. The tendrils snapped, losing their grip on Belly's belly, the skin puckering where they'd been connected. Each broken connection drove fresh, red-hot pain, through her belly.

Wincing, Beth pulled her feet out from under Isabel and, before the woman could do anything, quickly clambered over her legs.

Isabel tried to push Beth away, but the tendrils were still attached to her fingers and writhing, picking at the concrete. Beth slapped her face, her palm stinging, but the contact wasn't right, as if she were slapping heavy air.

Get off me," Isabel commanded. "You do not realise your actions."

Some of the tendrils crept towards Isabel, inching up her waist and towards Beth. She saw them and slapped them away, making Isabel cry out in pain each time.

"Let me go," she screamed and moved her body from side to side, trying to unseat Beth.

Caught off guard, Beth felt herself falling forwards. She knew, if that happened, that it would only be a matter of moments before Isabel was on top of her again, ready to penetrate her belly with the tendrils.

To steady herself, Beth pressed her hands on Isabel's belly.

Isabel howled in agony.

Beth looked down and felt the cold fingers of insanity clutching for her.

Her hands were dark on Isabel's pale skin, which had the texture of jelly. Beth blinked hard, twice, to make sure that what she was seeing was really happening.

Her fingertips were gone, buried into Isabel's belly. She could feel things squirming against them, like a million tiny insects and, with a cry of revulsion, pulled her hands away. They came free from Isabel's flesh with an audible pop and tendrils were attached, pulling at the woman's skin.

Repulsed, Beth leaned back and kicked at the floor, sliding down Isabel's legs. The tendrils stretched and pulsed, the green smoky colour of them growing weaker the further they were pulled.

When Beth felt Isabel's feet against her backside, she stood up and backed away unsteadily, shaking her hands furiously to try and free them from the tendrils. It was several steps before the first one grew darker and wispier, before snapping off and dropping onto Isabel's right foot, where it curled around her big toe and soaked into her skin.

A few more steps and all of the tendrils were severed. Beth sat down, shaking and sobbing uncontrollably. Through her tears, she could barely see Isabel, who was screaming and writhing on the floor now, the tendrils all over her, entering and coming back out, spraying dark blood and mucus across her pale skin, which grew more translucent by the moment.

Beth jumped as Rob put his arms around her shoulders and said something to her that she didn't hear.

She couldn't speak. The sobs had taken hold of her now, as she watched Isabel's ravaged form gradually fade away to nothing.

CHAPTER 18

THE FIRST POLICE CAR arrived at The Yard five minutes after Mandy Valentine had managed to convince someone to lend her their mobile phone. She and Jill were waiting on the pavement and the first policeman was out of the car before it had even stopped. He took one look at the women and got back into the car, to radio for an ambulance to be sent as soon as possible.

In the car, the women broke down and told the police everything, including the fact that two other people were still in the warehouse, along with their kidnapper. The driver called it in, requesting back-up, since the situation was more grave than had originally been thought.

At this time, a message was relayed to Chief Constable Terry Duncan, who was midway through a round of golf at the Great Weston course outside Heyton.

As soon as he heard the details, he broke off the game and went straight to the manager's office in the clubhouse. With the door firmly closed, he rang his boss and the mayor of Heyton, not bothering to apologise to either for disturbing them on a Sunday.

Six minutes after those calls, a municipal works van pulled up outside The Yard, accompanied by three plain-clothes officers in an unmarked Vectra. They took over the scene and proceeded to clear everyone out of The Yard, civilians and job alike.

Within nineteen minutes of Mandy's call, The Yard was sealed off and the council workers were attending to business at the memorial so delicate and important that screens had to be set up, blocking the view of their work from the pavement and fair.

~

Beth slowly came to, aware that she was lying down.

There was pain in her body and she thought, for an awful moment, that she hadn't really beaten Isabel Mundy after all, that it had been some kind of fevered dream her subconscious had conjured up.

She opened her eyes and saw plain ceiling tiles. The walls around her were pale green, windows to her left and right, blinds drawn across them. An insistent beeping came from somewhere to her right that she couldn't quite see.

She tried to sit up but it felt like her head would split apart and she quickly laid back.

"Hey," said a voice to her left, a voice that had never felt more warm and welcoming.

"Rob?"

"Yes, sweetheart." He put his left hand gently on her chest and rested his head on her shoulder. She felt his lips brush her cheek.

"The baby?"

"It's fine, you both are."

The relief she felt, to hear that, was almost overwhelming and she felt a tear run down her cheek.

"Where am I?"

"Heyton Infirmary. You need rest, they said, so they put you in a private ward. They won't even let the police talk to you."

"The police?"

"Uh huh, I've already spoken to them. Apparently, they're going to send someone to speak to you in the next few days, when the doctor says you should feel up to it."

"What about Isabel?"

"Who?" Rob sounded confused.

Beth tried to turn her head to look at him, but her neck and shoulders hurt too much. "Isabel Mundy. The woman from the warehouse."

"I don't..." She heard him rub his chin. "Bloody hell, I'd forgotten about her. Dark haired woman, wasn't she?"

"Yes. What happened to her?"

Rob chuckled nervously. "You know, I haven't got a clue. How weird is that? Until you said it, I couldn't even remember seeing her and I'm pretty sure I didn't say anything about her to the coppers."

"You can't remember her?"

"No. In fact, all I can remember is opening the door and seeing you and her on the floor."

Beth closed her eyes. "I can remember everything about her."

~

It was dark when Beth woke up again and the only light in the room was the dim glow of a lamp, next to an easy chair that Rob was sitting in, asleep. He was snoring softly.

She felt something in her belly, a slight movement and put her hand over it.

"Hey, Junior," she said quietly, "we've had a bit of a time of it, haven't we?" As if in response, she felt the movement again and smiled. "But we'll get through it."

Rob made a snuffling noise and moved in the chair, folding his arms. Content, Beth closed her eyes, ready to welcome back the warm embrace of sleep.

The door opened, but she ignored it. It would just be a nurse, come to check her vital signs and gone soon.

The door shushed closed and Beth heard the nurse come towards the bed, her footsteps sounding like bare, damp feet slapping lightly on the floor.

Beth opened her eyes, her scalp pulled drum tight. The room was darker now and, in the gloom, she couldn't immediately see anything. Slowly, too slowly, her eyes adjusted and she could see Rob, asleep in the chair.

But no nurse.

The bed jerked, as if someone had grabbed the end of it and Beth bit her lip. Surely it had to be over now, after what she'd done at the warehouse.

The bed jerked again and a hand slapped onto the metalwork by her feet. It was white and lined, the fingertips puckered as if they'd been wet too long. Beth tried to scream, but no sound escaped.

A second hand appeared and Beth felt the bed move slightly, away from the wall. A head appeared, dark hair plastered flat to the scalp.

"No," Beth whispered.

The hands strained, the bed moving further from the wall, until the head was over the metalwork.

"Hello, Beth," said Isabel Mundy, her face a ruin, her eye sockets empty. "I've come for your baby."

177

Beth sucked in air until her lungs hurt and screamed.

~

"Hey, hey," said a voice to her left, "you have to calm down."

Beth didn't recognise it, felt no warmth or safety within it and kept her eyes tightly shut. "Go away, leave me alone."

"No," said the voice firmly. "Just calm down or you'll hurt yourself or the baby, alright?"

"Don't take my baby, I won't let you take him."

"I'm not going to, Beth, I'm just checking on you."

Beth opened her eyes. The nurse's head was turned away, as she checked a machine. Satisfied, she looked at Beth.

For the briefest of moments, Beth saw Isabel Mundy staring at her and then the illusion was gone, replaced by the round, friendly face of the nurse.

"There now, that's better isn't it?"

She felt gooseflesh on her arms and tried to see past the nurse, to where Rob had been sleeping. But he wasn't there.

"I hope so," said Beth, "I really do."

ABOUT THE AUTHOR

Mark West was born in 1969 and lives in Northamptonshire with his wife Alison and their young son Matthew. Writing since the age of eight, he discovered the small press in 1998 and since then has had over seventy short stories published around the world. His first collection, *Strange Tales*, was published in 2003 whilst his debut novel, *In The Rain With The Dead*, appeared from Pendragon Press in 2005. His novelette *The Mill*, which Mark Morris called 'one of the most moving pieces of writing I have read in a long time', appeared in the acclaimed five-author collection *We Fade To Grey*, edited by Gary McMahon and was later published by Greyhart Press. *What Gets Left Behind*, his critically acclaimed chapbook from Spectral Press, sold out four months prior to publication.

West has two novellas coming from Pendragon Press and is currently working on a novel. He can be contacted through his website at www.markwest.org.uk or on Twitter @MarkEWest

In the Rain with the Dead
by
Mark West

"You hear people say that they were 'sitting on the edge of their seats'... That describes what it's like reading this book." — Future Fire

Ten years after the incident with the Ouija board, Nadia and Jim meet at a friend's funeral and fall in love again. This time, their love will be real and lasting. But their friend had raised from the dead a disciple of Satan named Magellan. When he smells the purity of Jim and Nadia's affection, his master orders him to rend and corrupt their love. Magellan obeys with relish.

In the Rain with the Dead is both a horror novel and a romance set in the tired English town of Gaffney. But be warned, this is not a vampire-lite paranormal romance. Satan's undead disciple is pure evil; there are a few very strong scenes indeed!

Available in Kindle and ePUB eBook editions

The Mill
by
Mark West

"… packed with more emotion and feeling than you could imagine would be possible in a story of this length." — The Ginger Nuts of Horror

"It is eerie and sometimes chokes you up to read, but read it you should." — TheNovelBlog.com

Michael struggles to come to terms with the death of his wife. He has visions of her calling to him, inviting him to the beyond.

At the Bereaved Partners' Group, he learns that he is not the only one left behind who can hear the departed beckon them… to the Mill.

This Greyhart Press eBook is a novelette: longer than a short story but brief enough to read in one sitting.

Available in paperback and eBook editions

RESTLESS SOULS:
3 dark fables
by
Thomas Rydder

Three paranormal stories of America's unwanted souls.

Available in paperback and eBook editions.

DO UNTO OTHERS

When the slick and his family leave the house he's been staking, The Limey makes his move. Should be easy to steal enough to pay for his rent and his habits.

With the slick and his family on vacation, there's no one living there, but the house is far from empty . . .

Still mourning the death of her brother, bullied at school, and resenting her absent father, Simona is desperate enough to use a Ouija board to connect with her dead brother. It's not long before the corpses of students start appearing at school . . .

SIMONA SAYS

COLORS

Didn't anyone ever tell you not to wear the colors of a biker gang you don't belong to?

And it's not only the living bikers you gotta watch out for . . .

About Greyhart Press

Talk to us on Twitter (@GreyhartPress)
or email (editors@greyhartpress.com)

Greyhart Press

Greyhart Press is an indie publisher of quality genre fiction: fantasy, science fiction, horror, and some stories that defy description.

We publish eBooks and print-on-demand paperbacks through online retailers. That's great for us and for you, because we don't have to worry about all that costly hassle of stock-holding and distribution. Instead we can concentrate on finding great stories AND giving some away for free!

Visit our free story promotion page today for no-strings-attached free downloads.

Would you like to read our eBooks for free?

If so, our READ… REVIEW… REPEAT… promotion is for you.

See our website for more details.
www.greyhartpress.com

If you enjoyed this book, please consider leaving an online review at Amazon, Goodreads, or elsewhere. Even if it's only a line or two, it would be very helpful and would be very much appreciated.

Thank you.